TOWER VORTX VIZION DUAL AIR FRYER OVEN COOKBOOK 2024

1001 Days Crispy and Healthy Dual Air Fryer Oven Recipes, Perfect Homemade Meals for Everyone

Copyright©2023 Henry Webster
All rights reserved. No part of this book may be reproduced or used in any manner without the prior written permission of the copyright owner, except for the use of brief quotations in a book review.
Printed by Amazon in the USA.
Disclaimer : Although the author and publisher have made every effort to ensure that the information in this book was correct at press time, the author and publisher do not assume and hereby disclaim any liability to any party for any loss, damage, or disruption caused by errors or omissions, whether such errors or omissions result from negligence, accident, or any other cause. this book is not intended as a substitute for the medical advice of physicians.

TABLE OF CONTENTS

INTRODUCTION 6

POULTRY RECIPES 9

Air Fryer Chicken Breast 9
The Best Breaded Fried Chicken Wings 9
Air Fryer Chicken Pot Pie 10
Reheat Fried Chicken In The Air Fryer 10
Air Fryer Chicken Kiev Balls 10
Crispy Air Fryer Chicken Wings 11
Air Fryer Chicken Cutlets 11
Air Fryer Bbq Chicken Pizza Rolls 12
Air Fryer Frozen Breaded Chicken Breasts ... 12
Garlic Parmesan Chicken 13
Easy Tennessee-style Chicken Wings With Corn & Slaw 13
Air Fryer Whole Roast Chicken 13
Naked Hot Air Fryer Southern Chicken Wings 14
Air Fryer Hot Wings 14
Air Fried Hot Wings 14
Air Fryer Lemon, Garlic Chicken With Crispy Feta 15
Air Fryer Chicken Wings 15
Air Fryer Sweet Chili Chicken Wings 16
Air Fryer Chicken Tenderloins 17
Air Fryer Parmesan Crusted Chicken 17
Air-fryer Everything Bagel Chicken Strips ... 18
Air Fryer Chipotle Chicken Meatballs 18
Teriyaki Chicken & Pineapple Skewers 18

FISH & SEAFOOD RECIPES 20

Air Fryer Cod 20
Air Fryer Garlic Butter Shrimp 20
Air Fryer Bang Bang Shrimp 21
Air-fryer Tuna & Potato Fritters With Mayo ... 21
Homemade Fish Fingers With Lemon & Thyme New Potatoes 22
Air Fryer Easy Fish Tacos 22
Air Fryer Shrimp 23
Sweet And Spicy Glazed Salmon 23
Air Fryer Lemon Garlic Shrimp 24
Air Fryer Prawns 24
Grilled Salmon With Fresh Salad & Grilled Corn 24
Vortex Air Fryer Fish & Chips 25
Air Fryer Catfish 25
Perfect Air Fryer Shrimp 26
Air Fryer Honey Sesame Salmon 26
Salmon With Roasted Miso Vegetables 27
Buttered Crab Rolls With Chive Mayo 28
Air Fryer Fish Sticks 28
Fish Taco Bowl 29
Air Fryer Tilapia 29
Air Fryer Scallops 30
Air Fryer Spicy Shrimp Fajitas 30
Crispy Coconut Shrimp 30

SANDWICHES & BURGERS RECIPES 32

Air Fryer Black Bean Burger 32	Cuban Sandwiches 35
Air Fried Black Bean Burger 33	Air Fryer Copycat Chick Fil A Sandwich 35
Air Fryer Turkey Burgers 33	Grilled Ham & Cheese Sandwiches 36
Air Fryer Hamburgers 34	Air Fryer Loose Meat Sandwiches 37
Air Fryer Grilled Cheese Sandwich 34	Minted Lamb Burgers 37

BEEF, PORK & LAMB RECIPES 38

Air Fryer Steak With Garlic-herb Butter 38	Air Fryer Roast Beef 42
Air Fryer Ham And Cheese Turnovers 38	Air Fryer Meatloaf 43
Air-fryer Pigs In Blankets 38	Bacon Wrapped Brussels Sprouts 43
Juicy Lucy Sliders 39	Air Fryer Copycat Taco Bell Crunchwrap 44
Air Fryer Top Round Roast 39	Air Fryer Brown Sugar Bacon Crackers 44
Peppercorn Steak Recipe 40	Air Fryer Bacon 44
Air-fryer Rosemary Sausage Meatballs 40	Air Fryer Bacon Wrapped Brussels Sprouts 45
Air-fryer Flank Steak And Fennel 40	Beef Stew 45
Reheat Steak In Air Fryer 41	Air Fryer London Broil 46
Air Fryer "shake 'n Bake" Style Pork Chops 41	Air Fryer New York Strip Steak 46
Air Fryer Flank Steak 42	Air Fryer Grilled Ham And Cheese 47

SALADS & SIDE DISHES RECIPES 48

Air Fryer Roasted Garlic & Rosemary Potatoes 48	Grilled Beets With Whipped Ricotta & Herbs 50
Air-fryer Brussels Sprouts Salad With Spiced Maple Vinaigrette 48	Salmon & Quinoa Salad 51
Air Fryer Garlic & Herb Potato Wedges 49	Air Fryer Chicken Milanese With Mediterranean Salad 51
Crispy Garlic, Scallion, & Sesame Potato Wedges 49	
Colcannon 49	Air Fryer Peppers And Onions 52
Warm Roasted Potato & Bacon Salad 50	Air Fryer Smashed Potatoes 52

VEGETABLE & & VEGETARIAN RECIPES 53

Spinach Artichoke Zucchini Bites 53	Air Fryer Corn On The Cob 55
Air Fryer Cauliflower Wings 53	Air Fryer Tofu 56
Air Fryer Broccoli 54	Air Fryer Fried Pickles 57
Air Fryer Spicy Cauliflower 54	Air-fryer Roast Potatoes Recipe 57
Air Fried Oyster Mushrooms 55	Air Fryer Radishes 57

Air Fryer Baked Potato 57	Air Fryer Vegetables 61
Air Fryer Twice Baked Potatoes 58	Air Fryer Buffalo Cauliflower 61
Air Fryer Roast Potatoes 58	Air Fryer Vegetable Peel Crisps 61
Air Fryer Pesto Roast Potatoes 59	Air Fryer Squash 62
Air Fryer Cheesy Potatoes 59	Air Fryer Brussels Sprouts 62
Air Fryer Stuffed Mushrooms 60	Roasted Brussels Sprouts With Pancetta 63
Air Fryer Veggie Tots 60	

FAVORITE AIR FRYER RECIPES 64

'pups' In Blankets With Sprouts 64	Crispy Air Fryer Pepper Rings 69
Air Fryer Frozen Mozzarella Sticks 64	Reheat Pizza In The Air Fryer 70
Air-fryer Mozzarella Sticks 65	Burst Tomato Cottage Cheese Caprese Bowl 70
Valentine's Day Air Fryer Pizza.................................65	Air Fryer Hot Dogs 70
Air Fryer Jalapeño Poppers 66	Air Fryer Crescent Mummy Dogs 71
Air Fryer Mozzarella Sticks 66	Hawaiian Pizza 71
Air Fryer Pizza 67	Air Fryer Fried Rice 71
Air Fryer Sweet Potato 67	Mummy Hotdogs 72
Air Fryer Tostones With Creamy Mojo Dipping Sauce 68	Latin Yellow Rice 72
Air Fryer Arancini 68	Air Fryer Smoked Sausage 73
Air Fryer Sausage, Peppers, And Onions 69	Air Fryer Wonton Mozzarella Sticks 73
	Air Fryer Frozen Pizza 74

SNACKS & APPETIZERS RECIPES 75

Air Fryer Snap Peas 75	Air Fryer Nachos 80
Air Fryer Sweet Potato Wedges 75	Sweet Potato Fries With An Air Fryer 80
Air-fryer Haloumi Popcorn With Maple Hot Sauce ... 76	Salt & Pepper Chilli Chips 81
Air-fryer Scallops With Lemon-herb Sauce 76	Air Fryer Zucchini Chips Recipe 81
Kids' Air-fryer Chickpea, Zucchini & Spinach Nuggets 77	Banana Chips 81
Air Fryer Breaded Asparagus Fries 77	Air Fryer Frozen Tater Tots 82
Air Fryer Asparagus Fries 78	Air Fryer Chips 82
Perfect Hot Chips 78	Air Fryer Tater Tots 83
Air Fryer Kale Chips 79	Dirty Fries 83
Air Fryer Fried Ravioli 79	Crispy Air Fryer Dill Pickles 84
Air Fryer Pickle Poppers 80	Ranch Cucumber Chips 84
	Air Fryer Zucchini Chips 85

BREAKFAST & BRUNCH RECIPES 86

- The Ultimate Cheese Toastie 86
- Cheesy Breakfast Egg Rolls 86
- Air Fryer Hard Boiled Eggs 86
- Air-fryer Bourbon Bacon Cinnamon Rolls 87
- Air Fryer Waffle Egg In A Hole 87
- Air Fryer Ranch Breadsticks 88
- Air Fryer Churros 88
- Air Fryer Boiled Eggs 89
- Air Fryer Baked Eggs 89
- Air Fryer Frozen Pizza Rolls 90
- Air Fryer Hash Browns 90
- Air Fried Pineapple Empanadas 90
- Air Fryer Cinnamon Rolls 91
- Air Fryer Potato Pancakes 91
- Air Fryer Garlic Bread 92
- Air Fryer Empanadas 92
- Sausage & Hash Brown Omelette 93
- Rustic Mediterranean Tomato Dip With Grilled Pita 93
- Air Fryer Zucchini Corn Fritters 94
- Air Fryer French Toast 94
- Air Fryer Soft Pretzels 95
- Air Fryer Pretzel Crescent Rolls 95
- Air Fryer Texas Toast 96

DESSERTS RECIPES 97

- Hot Cocoa Cookies 97
- Air Fryer Crab Cakes 97
- Air Fryer Apple Fritters 98
- Air Fryer Fried Apple Pies 99
- Homemade Bagels 99
- Air Fryer Basic Vanilla Butter Cookies 100
- Air Fryer Blueberry Cheesecake Wontons 100
- Air Fryer Cranberry Brie Bites 101
- Soufflé Pancakes With Berries & Cream 101
- Apple Cider Donuts 102
- How To Toast A Bagel In An Air Fryer 103
- Air Fryer Oven Slime-filled Cookies 103
- Crispy Air Fryer Apple Fritters 103
- Best-ever S'mores 104
- Peanut Butter Explosion Cakes 104
- Air Fried Cheese Curds 105
- Air Fryer Donuts 105
- Air Fryer Bagels 106
- Frozen Waffles In The Air Fryer 106
- Air Fryer Pecan Pie 107
- Chocolate Hot Cross Buns 107
- Red Velvet Cookies 108
- Carnival Fried Oreos 108

INTRODUCTION

Many people enjoy comfort foods like fried chicken wings and fries. However, eating such foods regularly can increase the risk of health conditions like heart disease and diabetes. In fact, research shows that eating fried foods can increase your risk of heart failure. If you love the taste of fried foods but want to forego the negative health effects, you might consider air fryers. But are they really a better choice? And do they really mimic fried foods? Read on to learn about the benefits of using an air fryer for cooking and the different foods you can prepare with it. An air fryer is basically a convection oven in a compact size that you can keep on your kitchen countertop. Air fryers allow food to cook evenly in less time than conventional ovens or toaster ovens. Air fryers cook food with the help of hot air. More specifically, when you put food into an air fryer, hot air will circulate around it. The perforations, or small holes on the air fryer pan, help circulate the hot air and assist with even cooking on both sides. Unlike deep frying, using an air fryer requires little to no oil. Rather, the hot air itself is enough to impart a crisp texture.

What are the potential benefits of using an air fryer?
There's a reason air fryers have taken off in popularity. A lot of it has to do with the potential health benefits, as opposed to traditional frying, and the convenience of using them.

Fried foods minus the health risks
Deep-fried foods absorb oil during the cooking process, resulting in a high-fat food. Fried foods are high in saturated and trans fats. These types of fats can damage the walls of your arteries, causing plaque buildup. This, in turn, narrows the arteries and makes it harder for blood to travel throughout the body. This is similar to what happens when a pipe gets clogged. When your arteries are clogged, it's called atherosclerosis. Atherosclerosis puts you at increased risk of heart disease. Air-fried foods, on the other hand, require much less oil (as little as 1 tbsp). So the food has a much lower fat content, and the health risks are significantly decreased. Air-fried foods also tend to have fewer calories than traditionally fried foods. This is because oil tends to add calories to food. This may matter if you are looking to lose weight.

Speed is on your side
Air fryers can also save you time. Protein-rich foods like meats, chicken, and seafood may have similar cooking times as the oven. However, some baked goods, like cake, can have faster cooking time with an air fryer than with an oven.
You can also save time if you need to reheat foods. The air fryer takes only 3 to 5 minutes to preheat, as compared to the 10 to 15 minutes it takes the typical oven to preheat.

Safer than deep frying
Deep frying foods can be very dangerous. The hot oil used in deep frying can reach 400 °F (204°C) and, if not contained correctly, can cause severe burns. And there's an added risk when this oil comes in contact with water. Water can cause the oil to splatter, increasing the risk of the hot oil burning you. Plus, the hot oil is extremely flammable; a brief encounter with flames can start a fire. When air frying, you don't use much oil, and the food is contained. There is also no open flame. So air fryers don't share the same risks as deep fryers.

Fewer dangerous compounds than deep-fried foods
Another concern with deep-fried foods is the potential risk of creating cancer-causing compounds, like acrylamide. Acrylamide is a chemical that forms when a food containing sugars and an amino acid (asparagine) is exposed to high-heat cooking methods (such as frying). People commonly expose themselves to acrylamide by eating fried potato products, such as french fries and potato chips.

One study found that by switching to air frying, people can lower the risk of having acrylamide in their food by up to 90%.

What are some easy things to cook in an air fryer?
There are hundreds of recipes you can find online for delicious entrees, sides, and snacks that you can prepare in an air fryer. And besides preparing foods, you can also reheat pre-prepared foods and leftovers. Read below to learn about some of the most common foods you can cook in an air fryer.

- Proteins
    - Chicken
    - Shrimp
    - Steak
    - Tofu
    - Crab
    - Salmon and other fish
    - Burgers
    - Pork like bacon or chops
    - Turkey breast
- Vegetables
    - Potatoes
    - Cauliflower
    - Brussels sprouts
    - Broccoli
    - Squash
    - Corn on the cob
- Appetizers
    - Jalapeño poppers
    - Cheese sticks
    - Toasted ravioli
    - Empanadas
    - Onion Rings
- Baked Goods
    - Mini Cakes
    - Falafel
    - Biscuits
    - Brownies
    - Doughnuts

What are some tips for beginners using an air fryer?
If you are new to using an air fryer, the following tips can help you start cooking.

Choose the right size
For a small household of one to two people, a 3-quart air fryer should do. For families of four or more, 5- to 6-quart air fryers would allow for larger batch cooking.

More expensive isn't necessarily better
Air fryers range in price from $30 to more than $600. But is there a big difference? Likely not when it comes to simply air frying. The reality is that all air fryers work the same way. Expensive versions tend to have more bells and whistles, but if simplicity is your thing, an affordable one should work just fine.

Place on a heat-resistant surface
The bottom of your air fryer will become hot during cooking and will take time to cool down. Therefore, make sure you place it on a heat-resistant surface like a granite or steel countertop. You can also place it on a heat-resistant silicone mat.

Always preheat before using
Preheat the air fryer for about five minutes at the temperature your air fryer instructions or recipe recommend. Your air fryer may have a manual temperature dial or digital buttons to allow you to adjust the temperature.

Don't overcrowd
When you are cooking in your air fryer, it's important not to place too much in your air fryer pan at one time. Place a single layer of protein or veggies to allow for fast and even cooking.

Shake things up
Giving your air fry basket a little shake will help ensure even cooking. This helps you avoid undercooking your food, which poses the risk of foodborne illness.

Clean after each use
If you don't clean your air fryer, old food particles and bacteria can build up and contaminate the food you put in it. To avoid this and ensure that your air fryer is working at its best, it's important to clean it after each use. Allow your air fryer basket or rack to cool before cleaning. Air fryers can provide a convenient and quick way to prepare healthier versions of your favorite fried foods. And the bonus is that you don't need to be a skilled cook to use an air fryer. Air fryers aren't the only option; roasting, baking, and steaming are other healthy cooking methods. And remember, the type of food you cook still matters. The key is to focus on a wide variety of nutritious, whole foods when it comes to healthy eating.

POULTRY RECIPES

Air Fryer Chicken Breast

Servings: 4
Cooking Time: 8 Minutes

Ingredients:
- 4 medium chicken breast fillets 4-6 ounces each
- 1 tablespoon olive oil
- 2 teaspoons smoked paprika
- 2 teaspoons cumin
- 1 teaspoon onion powder
- 1/2 teaspoon salt
- 1/2 teaspoon pepper

Directions:
1. Preheat the air fryer to 200C/400F.
2. Pat dry the chicken breasts then add them into a bowl and rub the oil generously over them all.
3. Add the spices in a bowl, then rub on both sides of the chicken breast fillets. If desired, let the chicken sit for 10 minutes.
4. Place the chicken breasts in the air fryer basket and cook for 4 minutes, flip, and cook for another 4-5 minutes, or until the chicken reaches an internal temperature of 165F.
5. Remove the chicken from the air fryer basket and serve immediately.

Notes
TO STORE: Leftovers can be stored in the refrigerator, covered, for up to five days.
TO FREEZE: Place the cooked and cooled chicken breasts in a ziplock bag and store them in the freezer for up to two months.
TO REHEAT: Microwave the chicken for 20-30 seconds or in the air fryer for 2-3 minutes.

The Best Breaded Fried Chicken Wings

Servings: 2
Cooking Time: 25 Minutes

Ingredients:
- 1 lb. chicken wings (approximately 10 pieces)
- 1 teaspoon olive oil
- 1 teaspoon soy sauce
- 1 teaspoon granulated sugar
- 1 teaspoon salt
- 1 teaspoon black pepper
- 1 teaspoon cayenne pepper (optional)
- 1 cup all-purpose flour (or panko breadcrumbs)
- 2 eggs, beaten
- vegetable oil
- GARLIC TOPPING (OPTIONAL)
- 1 tablespoon olive oil
- 1/4 cup garlic, chopped
- 1/2 tablespoon Italiano seasoning
- 1 teaspoon salt
- 2 small red chilli peppers, sliced (optional)

Directions:
1. Place chicken wings in a sealable Ziploc bag. Add olive oil, soy sauce, sugar, salt and pepper (and cayenne, if using) in the bag. Shake well to combine, press air out of the bag and seal tightly. Press the marinade around the chicken to fully coat. Place in the fridge and marinate for at least 1 hour, up to overnight.
2. Add flour in a shallow bowl. Add beaten egg in another shallow bowl. Roll the chicken wings in the flour, then dip in the eggs to fully coat, and then back in the flour once more.
3. Heat 1/8-inch of oil in a frying pan over medium heat for 3 minutes (I used about 1/4 cup in my large pan). Place the coated chicken wings in the pan and cook for 1 minute on each side until the flour coating turns light brown.

4. Remove from heat and place wings on a plate for 5 minutes to cool down, then place in the air fryer basket. (Note that 10 pieces of wings fit perfectly in the air fryer basket).
5. Cook at 350 F for 20 minutes. Open and shake the basket halfway through to make sure they cook evenly.
6. Prepare garlic topping (optional): Heat olive oil in a small frying pan over medium heat. Add garlic, Italiano seasoning, salt and chilli peppers, if using. Sauté for 1-2 minutes until garlic becomes fragrant. Remove from pan and drizzle on top of the chicken wings.

NOTES

Pre-cooking the wings in a pan: This will not only help create a crunchy outer breading but also make the breading stick well. You can choose to directly cook in the air fryer without pre-cooking in a pan but the breading tends to be flaky and come off easily.

How to serve: Wings are best served hot. You can reheat in the air fryer if needed.

Cooking in the oven: If you don't have an air fryer, you can bake in an oven at 425 F for 30-35 minutes.

Air Fryer Chicken Pot Pie

Servings: 4
Cooking Time: 15 Minutes

Ingredients:

- 1 ½ cups cooked chicken diced*
- 2 cups mixed frozen vegetables
- 10.5 ounce condensed cream of chicken soup or cream of celery
- ¼ cup milk
- ¼ teaspoon thyme
- ¼ teaspoon parsley
- salt and pepper to taste
- 4 biscuits Pillsbury biscuits +see note

Directions:

1. Preheat air fryer to 325°F.
2. Combine all ingredients in a bowl except for the biscuit dough. Mix until fully combined.
3. Divide the mixture into four ovenproof small ramekins or bowls and cook for 10 minutes.
4. After 10 minutes remove the basket and add a biscuit on top of each bowl.
5. Cook for 5-6 minutes or until the biscuit is cooked all the way through.

Notes

*Use only pre-cooked chicken that has reached a safe internal temperature of 165°F.

+ In order to use up a full can of 8 biscuits, the filling recipe can be doubled to make 8 individual servings.

Reheat Fried Chicken In The Air Fryer

Servings: 2-4
Cooking Time: 10 Minutes

Ingredients:

- Leftover fried chicken (4 to 6 pieces)

Directions:

1. Preheat your air fryer to 370 degrees F.
2. Place the chicken pieces in the basket of the air fryer. Make sure they are arranged in a single layer and don't overlap.
3. Cook for about 5 minutes, flip, and cook for an additional 5 minutes. Exact cooking time may vary depending on the size of your chicken pieces.
4. Remove with tongs, serve, and enjoy!

Air Fryer Chicken Kiev Balls

Servings: 2

Ingredients:

- 300 g chicken (breast or ground), (12oz)
- 3 cloves garlic, crushed
- 100 g breadcrumbs, (3/4 cup)
- 120 g butter, (1/2 cup)
- 2 fresh parsley sprigs
- 1 egg

Directions:

1. Mix together the butter, chopped parsley and crushed garlic. You can use a food processor to do

this, just don't over process it or the butter will go too soft.

2. Divide the butter out into 12 (ish) equal sized balls. Pop them in the fridge (or freezer if you are short on time), to harden up.
3. If you are using whole chicken breasts instead of already minced/ground meat then you will need to also run this through a food processor, or high speed blender.
4. Once your garlic butter balls have hardened up a little, it's time to start wrapping your ground chicken around them. Take a little bit of chicken at a time and wrap some around each butter ball as a thin layer, around 1 to 1.5cm.
5. Beat the egg in a bowl, ready to dip your chicken balls in. Set up another bowl with your breadcrumbs in. You can use day old bread and pop it in a food processor to turn it into small crumbs, or as I often like to do, keep some store bought breadcrumbs in the cupboard. Season your breadcrumbs depending on your tastes (salt, pepper, perhaps a little paprika if you want some extra flavour).
6. For the next step (and final part of the preparation!) I use some kitchen tongs. It makes it easier to dip the balls and ensure they are evenly coated all over. Firstly dip the ball in the egg bowl, then roll it around in the bowl of breadcrumbs. Make sure the breadcrumbs are holding on tight or the air fryer might blow them off. If need be use your hand to press them in firmer.
7. I sprayed them with a little oil (using an oil sprayer) and then placed them in my air fryer basket. I cooked them for 10 minutes at 200C/390F). Check half way through and turn over.

Notes

Side note: some people like to include some flour to this part of the process - they feel it helps the breadcrumbs hold to the meat better. I personally prefer to omit it (I don't notice a difference). If you want to include flour just dip the balls in the flour before the egg.

Crispy Air Fryer Chicken Wings

Servings: 4
Cooking Time: 20 Minutes

Ingredients:
- 1 pound split chicken wings tips removed
- 1 tablespoon vegetable oil
- salt & pepper to taste

Directions:
1. Preheat the air fryer to 400°F.
2. Toss wings with oil and generously season with salt & pepper.
3. Place in a single layer in the air fryer basket.
4. Cook 20-22 minutes flipping the wings after 10 minutes.
5. Toss with sauce if desired.

Notes

Do not overcrowd the air fryer or the wings won't crisp. If needed cook 2 batches and place all of the wings into the air fryer to heat together at the end.
If cooking in batches, the second batch will need about 2-3 minutes less.

Air Fryer Chicken Cutlets

Servings: 4
Cooking Time: 10 Minutes

Ingredients:
- 4 chicken cutlets
- 2 eggs
- 1/2 cup Italian breadcrumbs
- 1/2 tsp paprika
- 1/4 tsp garlic powder
- 1/4 tsp onion powder
- 1/8 tsp cayenne (optional)
- Salt and pepper to taste

Directions:
1. Season the chicken with salt and pepper.
2. In one small container whisk the eggs and in another combine the breadcrumbs and seasonings.
3. Preheat your air fryer to 400 degrees F.

4. Dredge your chicken cutlet in the eggs, flipping and covering each side. Then shake off any excess egg and lay it in the breadcrumbs, using your fingers to help completely cover the chicken. Flip and do the same to the other side. Shake off any excess breading. Continue to do this with the remaining chicken cutlets.
5. Spray your air fryer and lay two chicken cutlets in the basket. Cook for 10 to 12 minutes, flipping halfway through. Check the internal temperature to make sure it is at 165 degrees F. For my air fryer, 10 minutes was perfect, but all vary a little differently.
6. Serve and enjoy.

NOTES
HOW TO COOK PRE-COOKED FROZEN BREADED CHICKEN CUTLETS:
Preheat the air fryer to 380 degrees F.
Lay two frozen chicken cutlets in the basket and cook for 4 to 6 minutes, flipping halfway through until thoroughly heated.
HOW TO REHEAT CHICKEN BREAST CUTLETS:
Preheat the air fryer to 350 degrees F.
Place two leftover cutlets in the air fryer basket.
Cook for 4 to 5 minutes until heated through and crispy on the outside.

Air Fryer Bbq Chicken Pizza Rolls

Servings: 4
Cooking Time: 6 Minutes

Ingredients:
- 1 can Crescent Dough Sheet 8 ounces
- 1/2 cup BBQ Sauce
- 1/2 tsp garlic powder
- 1/2 tsp red pepper flakes
- 1 can precooked chicken 12.5 ounces
- 1 1/2 cup mozzarella cheese
- 4 slices cooked bacon crumbled
- 2 green onions chopped

Directions:
1. Lightly oil or use air fryer parchment paper liners to prepare the air fryer basket. Set aside.
2. Roll out the pastry sheet so that it is a true rectangle. Evenly brush the BBQ sauce on top of the sheet.
3. Season the sauce with the red pepper flakes and garlic powder, and then sprinkle mozzarella cheese over the sauce,
4. Drain the can of chicken and lightly shred any large chunks. Spread the chicken over the cheese.
5. Top the pizza with chopped onion and crumbled bacon, then, tightly roll the the dough lengthwise until it is a long roll.
6. Slice the roll into eight pieces and place in the air fryer basket, cut side down.
7. Air fry at 370 degrees F for about 5-6 minutes, until the crust is golden.

Air Fryer Frozen Breaded Chicken Breasts

Servings: 2
Cooking Time: 15 Minutes

Ingredients:
- 2 Frozen Breaded Chicken Breasts
- EQUIPMENT
- Air Fryer

Directions:
1. Place the frozen breaded chicken breasts in the air fryer basket in a single layer. Make sure they aren't overlapping. No oil spray is needed.
2. Air Fry at 380°F/193°C for 10 minutes. Flip the chicken over.
3. Continue to Air Fry at 380°F/193°C for another 2 minutes. Check the chicken breasts and if needed, add another 2-3 minutes or until heated through and crispy to your preference.

NOTES
Air Frying Tips and Notes:
No Oil Necessary. Cook Frozen - Do not thaw first.
Don't overcrowd the air fryer basket. Lay in a single layer.

Recipe timing is based on a non-preheated air fryer. If cooking in multiple batches of chicken back to back, the following batches may cook a little quicker.

Recipes were tested in 3.7 to 6 qt. air fryers. If using a larger air fryer, the chicken might cook quicker so adjust cooking time.

Remember to set a timer to flip/toss as directed in recipe.

Garlic Parmesan Chicken

Servings: 4

Ingredients:

- 4 bone-in, skin-on chicken thighs
- Kosher salt
- Freshly ground black pepper
- 1 c. Panko breadcrumbs
- 1 tsp. garlic powder
- 1 tsp. Italian seasoning
- 2/3 c. freshly grated Parmesan
- 2 large eggs

Directions:

1. Season chicken with salt and pepper. In a shallow bowl, whisk together panko, garlic powder, Italian seasoning, and Parmesan. In another shallow bowl, beat eggs.
2. Dip chicken thighs in egg, then roll in Panko mixture until fully coated.
3. Cook in air fryer at 360° for about 25 minutes or until golden and cooked through.

Easy Tennessee-style Chicken Wings With Corn & Slaw

Servings: 4
Cooking Time: 20 Minutes

Ingredients:

- 600g Woolworths Tennessee style chicken wing nibbles
- 450g Woolworths American bbq coleslaw
- 1kg frozen Australian corn cobs
- 1 spring onion, thinly sliced
- 1/3 cup whole egg mayonnaise (to serve)
- 1 lemon, cut into cheeks (to serve)

Directions:

1. Preheat air fryer to 180°C for 3 minutes. Place chicken in basket. Slide pan and basket into air fryer. Cook for 20 minutes, turning occasionally, or until golden and cooked through.
2. Meanwhile, prepare coleslaw according to packet instructions. Season.
3. Cook corn according to packet instructions.
4. Place chicken on tray and scatter over onion. Serve with coleslaw, corn, mayonnaise and lemon cheeks.

Air Fryer Whole Roast Chicken

Servings: 4-6
Cooking Time: 1 Hour

Ingredients:

- 1 whole chicken (up to 2kg, depending on the size of your air fryer)
- 1tbsp olive oil
- 1tsp smoked paprika
- 1tsp dried mixed herbs
- 1tsp garlic granules/salt

Directions:

1. Using a brush, coat the chicken in olive oil.
2. Mix the seasoning together and paste it all over the chicken. Make up some more spice mix if there isn't enough to coat the whole chicken.
3. Place the chicken in the air fryer basket, breast side down. Cook at 180°C for 45 minutes. Check on it once or twice to ensure it is cooking ok and not burning.
4. At 45 minutes, turn the chicken over so that it is breast side up. Cook for a further 15 minutes.
5. Check the chicken has cooked through. You can pierce it with a sharp knife to see if the juices run clear - or, my preferred way, use a meat thermometer to check the internal temperature. If it isn't cooked through, return it to the air fryer and cook for some more time, checking on it every so often.

Notes

Serve with chips, potato wedges, rice, salad - anything goes with chicken.

Experiment with different seasoning rubs, and you can change up the taste each time.

Naked Hot Air Fryer Southern Chicken Wings

Servings: 4
Cooking Time: 25 Minutes

Ingredients:

- ½ cup (1 stick) butter
- ⅓ cup Hot Sauce
- 2 pounds chicken wings, each wing cut at joint to yield wingette and drumette
- 2 tablespoons peanut oil
- 1 teaspoon Kosher salt
- ⅛ teaspoon cayenne pepper
- oil, for spraying

Directions:

1. To make buffalo sauce, in a small saucepan over medium heat, combine butter and The Lady & Sons Signature Hot Sauce and heat just until butter melts; keep warm on stovetop. Wash wings, pat dry, and place in a large bowl. Add peanut oil, salt, and cayenne pepper and toss to thoroughly coat wings.
2. Working in batches of 8, place wings in air fryer basket. Set temperature to 400 degrees, and air fry for 25 minutes. Shake occasionally, spraying with oil once during cooking. Repeat with remaining chicken.
3. In a large bowl, toss fried chicken in buffalo sauce, and remove with a slotted spoon to a serving dish.

Air Fryer Hot Wings

Servings: 2
Cooking Time: 22 Minutes

Ingredients:

- 1 pound chicken wings
- 1 tablespoon olive oil
- salt and pepper to taste
- ½ cup hot sauce

Directions:

1. Preheat air fryer to 400°F.
2. Toss wings with oil and seasoning in a bowl. Place in a single layer in the air fryer basket.
3. Cook for 20 minutes flipping the wing halfway through the cook time.
4. Toss wings with hot sauce and return to the air fryer basket cooking for 2 more minutes.

Notes

To cook frozen chicken wings: Separate from each other and air fry in stages, shaking the basket every 5 minutes. Sauce and finish cooking as normal.

Air Fried Hot Wings

Ingredients:

- Chicken Wings (around 10)
- 1/2 stick of butter
- 1/2 cup all-propose flour
- 1/4 tsp Paprika
- 1/4 tsp Cayenne pepper
- 1/4 tsp Salt
- dash of Black pepper
- dash of Garlic powder
- 1/4 cup of your favorite hot sauce

Directions:

1. In a small bowl, whisk together flour and spices.
2. Cover the chicken wings with the flour mixture.
3. Lightly drizzle oil over the coated chicken wings.
4. AirFry the wings for 10 minutes at 370°
5. Remove and give the wings a turn
6. Return to the AirFryer for another 5 minutes at 370°

7. In a saucepan, combine butter and Hot Sauce at mid-heat.
8. Let simmer until the butter is melted. Stir continuously.
9. Remove from heat.
10. In a mixing bowl, pour hot sauce over the cooked chicken wings and mix until thoroughly coated.
11. EAT!

Air Fryer Lemon, Garlic Chicken With Crispy Feta

Servings: 4
Cooking Time: 30 Minutes

Ingredients:
- 500g Chicken Thighs
- 1 Tablespoon Minced Garlic or Garlic Purée
- 2 Lemons
- 50g of Rice Per Person
- Feta Cheese
- Oil
- 1 Teaspoon of Chilli Flakes
- 1 Tablespoon of Flour

Directions:
1. Place chicken thighs in a bowl. Coat in the garlic, juice of 1 lemon, chilli flakes, plenty of oil and salt and pepper (best to do this at night or few hours before to let marinate). Add in flour before cooking and coat in that too.
2. Place in air fryer for 15 minutes on 200°C.
3. Cook rice, when cooked and drained, stir through a squeeze of lemon and a teaspoon of garlic.
4. For the crispy feta, cut up the slab of cheese into small squares. Coat them in flour, spray or drizzle with oil and place in air fryer.
5. Serve crispy chicken thighs with lemon rice and top with crispy feta and chilli flakes.

Air Fryer Chicken Wings

Servings: 4
Cooking Time: 25 Minutes

Ingredients:
- 1 pound chicken drumettes and flats
- salt and pepper to taste
- One homemade recipe of buffalo sauce (optional)

Directions:
1. Preheat air fryer to 380 degrees.
2. Trim or separate wings at the joint if needed, creating a flat and drumette per chicken wing. Discard the tips.
3. Pat chicken wings dry -- you will want them as dry as possible to help crisp them up.
4. Coat chicken wings with a generous amount of salt and a little pepper.
5. Cook wings at 380 degrees until cooked through, about 20-22 minutes shaking the basket or flipping wings halfway through.
6. Increase air fryer temperature to 400 degrees and cook until chicken wings get a nice crispy outside, about 4-5 minutes.
7. Coat with homemade buffalo sauce or other desired sauce.
8. Enjoy immediately.

NOTES

How to reheat chicken wings in the air fryer*:

Preheat air fryer to 350 degrees.

Cook chicken wings for 5-6 minutes until heated thoroughly.

Remove from the air fryer and enjoy!

*They will heat up better without sauce on them as different sauces will cook differently.

Air Fryer Sweet Chili Chicken Wings

Servings: 2
Cooking Time: 20 Minutes

Ingredients:

- Air Fryer Chicken Wings
- 12 Chicken Wings
- 1/2 Tbsp Baking Powder NOT BAKING SODA
- 1 Tsp Ground Black Pepper
- 1/2 Tsp Sea Salt
- 1 Tsp Garlic Powder
- 1/4 Tsp Onion Powder
- 1/4 Tsp Paprika
- Thai Sweet Chili Sauce
- 1 Tbsp Soy Sauce
- 1 1/2 Tbsp Hoisin Sauce
- 3 1/2 Tbsp Sweet Chili Sauce
- 1/2 Tbsp Rice Wine Vinegar
- 1/2 Tbsp Sesame Oil
- 1 Tbsp Brown Sugar Optional
- 2 Cloves Garlic Minced
- 1/2 Tsp Ground Ginger
- 1/4 Tsp Sea Salt
- 1/2 Tbsp Lime Juice
- 1/4 Cup Water
- Sriracha Ranch Dip
- 1/3 Cup Homemade Buttermilk Ranch Dressing Or your favorite store bought brand
- 1 Tbsp Sriracha
- 1/4 Tsp Cayenne Pepper
- Optional Garnish
- Sesame Seeds
- Lime Juice
- Sliced Green Onion
- Cilantro

Directions:

1. Crispy Chicken Wings
2. Dab chicken wings with a paper towel to ensure they are dry. Add the chicken wings to a zip-lock bag with baking powder and spices. Close the bag (making sure all the air is out) and toss everything together until the wings are coated.
3. Spray the metal rack (or basket) insert with cooking spray and arrange the chicken wings in a single layer. Close the Ninja Foodi lid and hit AIR CRISP, then set the TEMP to 400 degrees F, then set the TIME to 20 minutes and hit START. While the chicken wings are cooking make the sweet chili sauce.
4. *See Recipe Notes for oven instructions!
5. At 10 minutes open the lid and toss/flip the chicken wings with tongs to avoid them from sticking. Close the lid and allow them to cook for the remaining 10 minutes.
6. Once the time has expired check the internal temperature to ensure they are cooked though. Allow them to rest for 5 minutes before tossing in the sweet chili sauce.
7. Sweet Chili Sauce
8. Combine all ingredients into a small saucepan and heat over medium heat on the stove. Bring the sauce to a boil then reduce heat to a simmer stirring until the sauce has reduced and has slightly thickened. Keep sauce warm until chicken wings are finished.
9. Toss or dip the cooked chicken wings in the sauce. I like to make sure they are thoroughly coated.
10. Place the sauced chicken wings in a single layer on a greased cookie sheet with wire rack insert. Broil the chicken wings on the top rack on HIGH for 2-4 minutes. Stick close to the oven and check the wings often, they can burn quickly! Once the sauce is sticky and the wings have some color remove them from the oven. Serve warm with optional garnishes and Sriracha Ranch.
11. Sriracha Ranch Dip
12. Combine all ingredients in a small bowl and stir to combine. Serve with warm Sweet Chili Chicken Wings.

Notes

Leftover Storage: Store leftover chicken wings in an airtight container in the fridge for up to 4 days. Rewarm in the microwave until warmed through.

Oven Option: Follow recipe instructions for chicken wing prep. When ready to cook, heat oven to 425 degrees F and arrange wings in a single layer on a greased cookie sheet with a wire rack insert. Cook wings for 40 minutes (flipping halfway though) or until cooked through. Follow the recipe instructions for Sweet Chili Sauce and broiling the sauced wings.

Air Fryer Notes: I use the Ninja Foodi air fryer for this recipe. If you have a different air fryer that is fine, but the cook time and settings may vary. You may need to cook the chicken wings more or less depending on your air fryer. Please check them to make sure they are completely cooked through before eating. Also, if you have a smaller air fryer (mine is 5 quarts) you may need to cook the wings in multiple batches.

Air Fryer Chicken Tenderloins

Servings: 8

Cooking Time: 7 Minutes

Ingredients:

- 1 lb chicken tenderloins
- 2 tablespoons olive oil
- 1 teaspoon smoked paprika
- 1 teaspoon Italian seasoning
- 1/2 teaspoon garlic powder
- 1/2 teaspoon salt

Directions:

1. Preheat the air fryer to 190C/375F. Lightly grease the air fryer basket.
2. In a mixing bowl, add the chicken tenders and oil and mix well. Add the seasonings and mix until combined.
3. Add the chicken tenders to an air fryer basket in a single layer. Air fry for 7-8 minutes, flipping halfway through.
4. Remove the tenderloins from the air fryer basket and let them rest for 5 minutes before serving.

Notes

TO STORE: Place the cooked and cooled chicken in an airtight container and store it in the refrigerator for up to 4 days.

TO FREEZE: Keep them in an airtight container or freezer-safe bags and freeze for up to 3 months.

TO REHEAT: You can reheat them back in the air fryer, a preheated oven, or a hot skillet. You can also microwave them if you are in a time crunch.

Air Fryer Parmesan Crusted Chicken

Servings: 2

Cooking Time: 16 Minutes

Ingredients:

- 2 8 oz Boneless skinless chicken breast
- 2 tablespoon sour cream
- 1/4 cup Italian Style Panko Crumbs
- 1/4 cup grated parmesan cheese
- 1/2 teaspoon paprika
- 1/4 teaspoon salt
- 1/4 teaspoon pepper
- 1 tablespoon olive oil

Directions:

1. Preheat the air fryer to 380 degrees Fahrenheit.
2. Rinse and pat dry each piece of chicken.
3. Coat each piece of chicken with one tablespoon of sour cream or Greek yogurt, only covering the tops of the chicken.
4. In a medium bowl, combine the panko, parmesan cheese, and seasonings.
5. Pat the cheese mixture into the sour cream.
6. Lightly spray or brush the olive oil onto the basket.
7. Place the chicken into the basket and cook at 380 degrees F for 12 minutes.
8. Turn the chicken over and return to fryer to cook for an additional 4-6 minutes, depending on the thickness of the chicken.

Air-fryer Everything Bagel Chicken Strips

Servings: 4
Cooking Time: 15 Minutes

Ingredients:
- 1 day-old everything bagel, torn
- 1/2 cup panko bread crumbs
- 1/2 cup grated Parmesan cheese
- 1/4 teaspoon crushed red pepper flakes
- 1/4 cup butter, cubed
- 1 pound chicken tenderloins
- 1/2 teaspoon salt

Directions:
1. Preheat air fryer to 400°. Pulse torn bagel in a food processor until coarse crumbs form. Place 1/2 cup bagel crumbs in a shallow bowl; toss with panko, cheese and pepper flakes. (Discard or save remaining bagel crumbs for another use.)
2. In a microwave-safe shallow bowl, microwave butter until melted. Sprinkle chicken with salt. Dip in warm butter, then coat with crumb mixture, patting to help adhere. In batches, place chicken in a single layer on greased tray in air-fryer basket.
3. Cook 7 minutes; turn chicken. Continue cooking until coating is golden brown and chicken is no longer pink, 7-8 minutes. Serve immediately.

Air Fryer Chipotle Chicken Meatballs

Servings: 2-4

Ingredients:
- 1 lb. ground chicken (93% lean)
- 3/4 c. panko bread crumbs
- 1/4 c. chopped fresh cilantro
- 1 large egg, beaten
- 3 cloves garlic, minced
- 1 tbsp. finely chopped chipotle chiles in adobo sauce, plus 2 tsp. sauce
- 3/4 tsp. dried oregano
- 3/4 tsp. kosher salt
- 1/4 tsp. freshly ground black pepper
- Olive oil cooking spray
- Salsa verde, for serving

Directions:
1. In a medium bowl, using your hands, mix ground chicken, panko, cilantro, egg, garlic, chipotle chiles and sauce, oregano, salt, and pepper until combined. Roll into 1" balls.
2. Lightly coat an air-fryer basket with cooking spray. Working in batches, arrange meatballs in basket, spacing about 1/2" apart. Cook at 370°, turning a few times, until outsides of meatballs are golden brown and centers are cooked through, about 6 minutes.
3. Arrange meatballs on a platter. Spoon salsa verde over top or serve alongside for dipping.

Teriyaki Chicken & Pineapple Skewers

Servings: 4
Cooking Time: 12 Minutes

Ingredients:
- 3 large Boneless Skinless Chicken Breasts (cut into cubes)
- 1 pineapple (cut into cubes, the size of the chicken cubes)
- Bamboo skewers (cut to fit your air fryer basket)
- Sesame seeds, for topping (optional)
- Spring onion (for garnish)
- Teriyaki Sauce
- ½ cup soy sauce
- ¼ cup brown sugar
- 2 tbsp chilli oil
- 2 tbsp minced garlic
- 2 tsp minced ginger
- 2 tbsp Teriyaki sauce
- Slurry for Sauce
- 2 tbsp Cold Water
- 2 tbsp Corn-flour

Directions:

1. In a clean saucepan, over medium low heat, stir together the teriyaki sauce ingredients. Add in the slurry and allow to cook until it thickens. This will take just a few minutes.
2. Use two thirds of the sauce to marinate the chicken. Reserve the one third to brush over the chicken after it has been cooked. Allow chicken to marinate for 30 minutes in the fridge.
3. Make the skewers by adding and alternating with pineapple chunks and chicken.
4. Coat the air fryer tray with cooking oil.
5. Add a single layer of chicken skewers to the basket. Set the temperature of the Vortex to 200 degrees Celsius and the timer to 6 minutes. Flip and cook for another 4-6 more minutes until chicken is cooked through and the sauce has lightly caramelised on the outside.
6. Use reserved sauce for topping the chicken and sprinkle with sesame seeds and chopped spring onion.
7. Enjoy!

FISH & SEAFOOD RECIPES

Air Fryer Cod

Servings: 4
Cooking Time: 10 Minutes

Ingredients:
- 4 cod loins
- 4 tablespoons butter, melted
- 6 cloves of garlic, minced
- 2 tablespoons lemon juice (1 lemon)
- 1 teaspoon dried dill (or 2 tablespoons fresh dill, chopped)
- 1/2 teaspoon salt

Directions:
1. Preheat your air fryer to 370 degrees.
2. Mix the butter, garlic, lemon juice, dill, and salt in a bowl.
3. Add a cod loin into the bowl coating it completely. Lightly press the garlic into the cod so it doesn't fall off when cooking. Repeat with remaining cod pieces.
4. Place all the cod loins into the air fryer in one layer not touching.
5. Cook for 10 minutes then carefully remove from the air fryer.
6. Garnish the cod with more lemon juice or butter if desired and enjoy!

NOTES
HOW TO COOK FROZEN COD IN THE AIR FRYER:
Quickly rinse the cod in cold water for a second. Shake them over and place in a cold air fryer.
Turn the air fryer to 350 degrees and cook for 4 minutes.
Remove from the air fryer and follow ingredient and cooking instructions above like it is fresh cod!
HOW TO REHEAT COD IN AN AIR FRYER
Place the cod into an air fryer and turn to 350 degrees. Cook for about 5 minutes, until warmed, then enjoy!

Air Fryer Garlic Butter Shrimp

Servings: 4
Cooking Time: 8 Minutes

Ingredients:
- 1 pound shrimp peeled and de-veined
- 1/4 cup unsalted butter
- 2 cloves garlic minced, about 1 teaspoon

Directions:
1. After removing the shells, rinse the shrimp and pat them dry. Place them in a large bowl, and set aside.
2. In a small microwave safe bowl, combine the butter and minced garlic, and microwave for about 30 seconds, until the butter has melted.
3. Pour the butter and garlic mixture over the shrimp, and stir together, coating the shrimp with the mixture.
4. Pour the shrimp into the basket, leaving enough room between them so they aren't stacked.
5. Air fry at 370 degrees Fahrenheit for 6-8 minutes, tossing halfway through.
6. To determine doneness, the base of the shrimp tail will be an opaque color, and no longer translucent.

NOTES
Serve with melted butter or cocktail sauce, or on top of your favorite pasta.
KETO C/1 P/23 F/13
Weight Watchers: under 5 points per serving

Air Fryer Bang Bang Shrimp

Servings: 6
Cooking Time: 10 Minutes

Ingredients:
- Shrimp breading and seasoning
- 25 shrimp
- 1 egg
- 1 cup milk
- 3/4 cup all purpose flour
- 1/2 cup panko breadcrumbs
- 1/2 teaspoon red pepper
- 1/2 teaspoon ground black pepper
- 1/4 teaspoon onion powder
- 1/4 teaspoon garlic powder
- 1/4 teaspoon dried basil
- 1 Tablespoon olive oil to spray
- Bang Bang Sauce
- 1/2 cup mayo
- 4 teaspoons garlic chili sauce
- 1/2 teaspoon rice vinegar

Directions:
1. Clean shrimp thoroughly, then pat dry with paper towels.
2. Add panko bread crumbs, flour, and seasonings to a medium bowl. Mix well.
3. In a small mixing bowl, add egg to the milk and whisk until combined.
4. Dip the shrimp into the flour and panko mixture, the egg mixture, and then back into the flour mixture.
5. Set the coated shrimp on a cooling rack while finishing with the remainder of the shrimp.
6. Once all of the shrimp are coated, place the rack with the breaded shrimp into the refrigerator to chill for 30 minutes.
7. While the shrimp are chilling, make the spicy sauce. Add the mayo, chili garlic sauce, and rice vinegar to a small bowl. Mix well until thoroughly combined.
8. Preheat the air fryer to 400 degrees Fahrenheit (200 degrees Celcius)
9. Place shrimp in a single layer in the air fryer basket and lightly spray with olive oil. Leave room between the shrimp in the basket so the hot air can circulate evenly.
10. Air fry the shrimp for 5 minutes at 400 degrees Fahrenheit (200 degrees Celcius), carefully flip, lightly spray with olive oil, and cook for an additional 3-5 minutes until the shrimp are golden brown with a crispy coating. Cook the shrimp in batches if needed.
11. Carefully remove the shrimp from the air fryer basket and add to a shallow bowl.
12. Take 1/4 cup of the spicy sauce and add it to the bowl to coat shrimp. Save the leftover spicy sauce for dipping.
13. Serve immediately.

NOTES
This recipe was made using a 5.8 qt Cosori air fryer.
For dipping, you can use hot sauce, spicy ranch, Thai sweet chili sauce, sriracha sauce, or any other delicious sauce you like.
If you want to cut back on fat, swap out mayo for Greek yogurt. Plus, Greek yogurt has protein, so it's a win-win!

Air-fryer Tuna & Potato Fritters With Mayo

Servings: 4
Cooking Time: 30 Minutes

Ingredients:
- 425g John West tuna light in springwater, drained well
- 475g Woolworths classic potato mash
- 1 free range egg, beaten
- 1 1/2 cups panko breadcrumbs
- 5ml extra virgin olive oil cooking spray
- 300g Woolworths mixed leaf with carrot salad mix
- 1/3 bottle 400g Hellmann's real mayonnaise squeeze

Directions:

1. To a large bowl, add tuna, mashed potato, egg and panko. Season well and stir until thoroughly combined, adding more panko if necessary to ensure that mixture isn't too sticky.
2. Shape mixture into 12 evenly sized fritters. Spray a large air-fryer basket with oil.
3. Place half of the fritters in the basket. Cook at 200°C for 15 minutes, turning fritters and spraying with oil halfway through, or until golden. Transfer to a papertowel-lined plate. Repeat with remaining oil and fritters.
4. Divide fritters and salad mix amongst plates. Serve with mayonnaise.

Homemade Fish Fingers With Lemon & Thyme New Potatoes

Servings: 4

Ingredients:
- 400g chunky cod fillets
- 50g plain flour
- Zest of 1 lemon, divided
- Salt and pepper
- 1 large egg, beaten
- 50g dried breadcrumbs
- Spray oil
- For the potatoes
- 500g new potatoes, with skins on
- 2 tbsp olive oil
- 1 tbsp lemon juice
- 1 tbsp fresh thyme leaves OR
- 1 tsp dried thyme
- 1 garlic clove, crushed
- Sea salt flakes and pepper
- To serve
- For garnish Lemon wedges and parsley
- To serve peas and tartar sauce
- COOKING MODE
- When entering cooking mode - We will enable your screen to stay 'always on' to avoid any unnecessary interruptions whilst you cook!

Directions:
1. Remove skin from fillets. Cut cod into chunky strips about 2.5cm x 10cm
2. Prepare three shallow bowls for coating the fingers. One plate with flour, half the lemon zest and seasoning mixed together. One plate with egg, and one with breadcrumbs
3. Dip the cod fingers first in flour mixture, then in egg, and finally in the breadcrumbs. Insert crisper plate in both drawers and spray zone 1 drawer plate with oil. Place fish fingers in drawer. Spray with oil
4. If potatoes are too big, cut in half. In a bowl, put olive oil, lemon juice, lemon zest, thyme, garlic and salt. Add potatoes, toss to ensure they are thoroughly coated in oil mixture. Add potatoes to zone 2 drawer and insert both drawers into unit
5. Select zone 1, select AIR FRY, set temperature to 210°C, and set time to 15 minutes. Select zone 2, select ROAST, set temperature to 180°C and set time to 20 minutes. Select SYNC. Press the START/STOP button to begin cooking. When zone 1 and 2 reaches 10 minutes, turn fishfingers over and give potatoes a shake. When cook time is finished, use silicone coated tongs to remove food to a serving dish
6. Serve immediately with salad, tartar sauce, garnished with lemon wedges and parsley

Air Fryer Easy Fish Tacos

Servings: 8
Cooking Time: 6 Minutes

Ingredients:
- ½ cup mayonnaise
- 2 teaspoons adobo sauce from canned chipotle peppers
- 4 tilapia fillets (5 ounces each)
- 1 tablespoon House Seasoning
- oil, for spraying
- 8 corn tortillas
- ¼ head Savoy cabbage, shredded
- salt, to taste

- pepper, to taste

Directions:
1. In a small bowl, whisk together mayonnaise and adobo sauce. Set aside.
2. Working in batches of 2, season tilapia fillets on both sides with House Seasoning, spray fillets on both sides with oil, and place in air fryer basket. Set temperature to 350 degrees, and air fry for 6 minutes. Turn fillets and spray with oil halfway through cooking. Remove fillets to a plate and flake into chunky pieces with a fork. Repeat with remaining tilapia fillets.
3. Spread mayonnaise mixture on tortillas and top with fish and cabbage. Season with salt and pepper before serving.

Air Fryer Shrimp

Servings: 4
Cooking Time: 6 Minutes

Ingredients:
- 1 lb shrimp peeled and deveined, uncooked
- 2 tbsp olive oil
- 1 tsp garlic powder
- 1 tsp Italian seasoning
- ½ tsp chili powder

Directions:
1. After removing the shells, rinse the shrimp and pat them dry. Place them in a large bowl, and set aside.
2. In a medium bowl, toss shrimp with olive oil and then add seasonings and toss with shrimp until they are seasoned.
3. Pour the shrimp into the basket, leaving enough room between them so they aren't stacked.
4. Air fry at 370 degrees Fahrenheit for 6-8 minutes, tossing halfway through.
5. To determine doneness, the base of the shrimp tail will be an opaque color, and no longer translucent.

NOTES

Variations

Change up the seasoning - I think that adding Old Bay seasoning to this air fryer shrimp recipe sounds like a great addition to the recipe card. You can also kick up the heat and use some cajun seasoning or add some extra black pepper to this crispy air fryer shrimp. The perfect shrimp is going to be seasoned however you want it to be!

Use smaller shrimp - You can make this recipe with popcorn shrimp and medium sized shrimp, too. The shrimp size may change the cooking time, so be aware of that. Also, be sure that you use deveined shrimp to save yourself prep time!

Sweet And Spicy Glazed Salmon

Servings: 4
Cooking Time: 10 Minutes

Ingredients:
- 1 pound wild salmon filets (cut in 4 pieces)
- kosher salt
- 1/4 cup sweet red chili sauce
- 1 teaspoon Sriracha sauce
- 1/2 teaspoon fresh grated ginger
- sliced scallions (for garnish)

Directions:
1. Preheat oven to 400F. Spray a sheet pan with olive oil and set aside.
2. Place salmon on the sheet pan and season with 1/4 teaspoon salt.
3. In a small bowl combine red chili sauce sauce, sriracha and ginger. Brush over the salmon.
4. Roast in the oven 400F 8 to 10 minutes. Garnish with scallions.
5. Air Fryer Directions:
6. Air fry 400F 7 to 8 minutes.

Air Fryer Lemon Garlic Shrimp

Servings: 4

Cooking Time: 15 Minutes

Ingredients:

- 16 oz jumbo shrimp frozen, deveined
- 3 Tablespoon butter unsalted
- 2 teaspoon Italian seasoning
- 3 garlic cloves minced
- ¾ teaspoon old bay seasoning
- 2 Tablespoon fresh lemon juice sliced lemon pieces too
- ¼ teaspoon red pepper flakes
- Salt and pepper to taste

Directions:

1. Place ingredients in a container. Air fryer 350 degrees for 12-15 min, stirring halfway or until shrimp is translucent.

Notes

You can use frozen shell-on or peeled shrimp that has been deveined. Frozen shell-on shrimp does tend to be a little juicer.

If using defrosted shrimp, reduce the time until shrimp is fully cooked

Make a foil sling around the container so that it is easy to remove from the air fryer.

I prefer jumbo shrimp in this recipe but any size will work. Smaller shrimp cook faster so keep an eye on them.

Air Fryer Prawns

Servings: 4

Ingredients:

- 35g Plain Flour
- 3/4 tsp Garlic Granules
- 1/2 tsp Smoked Paprika
- 1/2 tsp Cayenne
- 1/2 tsp Salt
- 35g Breadcrumbs
- 30g Panko Breadcrumbs
- 2 Eggs, beaten
- 300g Prawns, shelled
- Cooking spray
- COOKING MODE
- When entering cooking mode - We will enable your screen to stay 'always on' to avoid any unnecessary interruptions whilst you cook!

Directions:

1. Combine flour with 1/2 tsp Garlic, 1/4 tsp Smoked Paprika, 1/4 tsp Cayenne and 1/4 tsp Salt in a bowl.
2. Combine both breadcrumbs with 1/4 tsp Garlic, 1/4 tsp Smoked Paprika, 1/4 tsp Cayenne and 1/4 tsp Salt in another bowl.
3. Preheat air fryer to 200C.
4. Toss Prawns in the flour mixture.
5. Then dip individually in egg and then breadcrumbs.
6. Repeat with remaining Prawns.
7. Lightly spray with cooking spray.
8. Add a single layer of Prawns to the air fryer basket.
9. Cook for 3 minutes.
10. Flip the Prawns and spray with more oil.
11. Cook for a further 2 – 3 minutes or until just cooked.
12. Repeat with remaining Prawns.

Grilled Salmon With Fresh Salad & Grilled Corn

Servings: 2

Ingredients:

- For the salmon
- 2 pieces of salmon, or any other dish you like
- For the marinate
- 4 tbsp olive oil
- 1 garlic clove or 1/2 tsp powdered garlic
- A pinch dried dill
- A pinch chilli flakes
- Salt and pepper
- 1/2 lemon juice
- For the salad
- Fresh leafs, baby leafs, salad
- Cherry tomatoes
- Rocket

- 2 Corn on the cob, cooked
- COOKING MODE
- When entering cooking mode - We will enable your screen to stay 'always on' to avoid any unnecessary interruptions whilst you cook!

Directions:
1. To make marinate, mix all ingredients together until well combined.
2. Using the brush, brush the fish with the marinate and set aside for a few minutes.
3. In the meantime heat up the grill. It will take about 8min
4. Once the grill it's ready, place the fish in, set the max temperature and 10 min time
5. Half way grilling add the corn and then the fish.
6. Grill until the time it's over. If you want your corn more charred, just grill it for additional 3-5 min
7. Serve with fresh salad, sprinkled with olive oil.

Vortex Air Fryer Fish & Chips

Ingredients:
- 5 pieces hake from frozen (easier to work with)
- 1 teaspoon paprika
- 1/2 teaspoon chilli powder
- 1/2 teaspoon chilli flakes
- 1/2 teaspoon jeera powder
- 1/2 teaspoon garlic powder
- 1/2 teaspoon lemon pepper
- 1/2 teaspoon dried parsley
- 1/2 lemon juiced
- 2 tablespoons oil
- For the star of the show, the sauce:
- 1/4 cup cream
- 1/2 cup melted butter
- 1 garlic clove chopped into teeny tiny pieces
- 1/2 lemon squeezed
- 1 teaspoon dried parsley
- Dash of aromat
- Salt and pepper to taste

Directions:
1. Mix all ingredients (besides fish) in a bowl.
2. With a silicone brush, brush your fish with the spice baste on both sides.
3. Place in air fryer gently. Set to 205c for 10 minutes. Turn, use silicone brush to brush any remaining oil/spices on fish. Air Fry for another 5 minutes. Remove with a spatula very gently.
4. In a small pot on medium heat add in your butter and chopped garlic, allow garlic to infuse with butter for a few seconds. Remove from heat.
5. In a bowl add in cream and squeezed lemon. Place pot back onto stove, slowly add cream mixture whilst whisking continuously. Add in aromat, salt and pepper.
6. Pour over fish, serve with chips. Enjoy!

Air Fryer Catfish

Servings: 2
Cooking Time: 20 Minutes

Ingredients:
- 2 catfish fillets
- 1 cup milk (or buttermilk)
- ½ tablespoon olive oil
- 1 ½ tablespoons blackening seasoning (or Cajun seasoning)
- ½ teaspoon dried oregano
- ½ teaspoon kosher salt
- ½ teaspoon black pepper
- ½ teaspoon garlic powder
- ¼ teaspoon cayenne pepper
- Lemon wedges, for serving
- Fresh chopped parsley, for garnish

Directions:
1. At least 30 minutes before cooking, place the catfish fillets in a plastic zipper bag or large bowl and pour the milk (or buttermilk) over it, allowing it to soak to remove the fishy flavor.
2. In a small bowl, combine the blackening or Cajun seasoning, oregano, salt, pepper, garlic powder, and cayenne pepper then set it aside.
3. When ready to cook, preheat your air fryer to 400 degrees. Remove the fish and pat it dry. Drizzle the

fillets with olive oil. Sprinkle the spice mixture onto both sides of each fillet, coating them completely.
4. Place the fillets in a single layer inside. Spray the tops of the fish.
5. Air fry at 400 degrees F for 10 minutes. Carefully flip the fish and fry for another 10 to 12 minutes (20 to 22 minutes total), until it reaches your desired doneness. Serve with lemon wedges and garnished with parsley.

NOTES
HOW TO REHEAT AIR FRYER CATFISH:
Place leftover fillets in the air fryer.
Air fry at 400 degrees for 4 minutes, until warmed through.
HOW TO COOK AIR FRYER CATFISH FROM FROZEN:
Ideally, you want to soak your catfish in the milk before freezing. If this is not possible, it can still be done while frozen, just soak it for an hour in room temperature milk, which will also help thaw it. If you do this, follow the directions as written.
If skipping the milk soak, skip directly to steps 2 and Preheat the air fryer to 400 degrees F. Then, air fry the fish for 13 minutes, flip and fry an additional 13 to 15 minutes (26 to 28 minutes total), until fully cooked.

Perfect Air Fryer Shrimp

Servings: 4
Cooking Time: 6 Minutes

Ingredients:
- 2 tablespoon extra-virgin olive oil
- 3/4 teaspoon garlic powder
- 3/4 teaspoon sweet paprika
- 3/4 teaspoon dried parsley
- 1/4 teaspoon kosher salt
- 32 jumbo peeled and deveined shrimp ((1 ¼ pounds))
- Lemon wedges (for serving)

Directions:
1. Mix oil with spices in a medium bowl.
2. Add the shrimp and mix well with the seasoning mixture on both sides to coat.
3. Arrange shrimp in air fryer basket in a single layer, in batches as needed.
4. Air fry 400F for 5 to 6 minutes, shaking the basket halfway.
5. Serve with lemon wedges.

Air Fryer Honey Sesame Salmon

Servings: 4
Cooking Time: 10 Minutes

Ingredients:
- 1 tablespoon sesame oil
- 1/4 cup honey
- 1 tablespoon sriracha
- 2 tablespoon soy sauce
- 3 cloves of garlic, minced
- Black pepper, freshly ground, to taste
- Salt, to taste
- 4 salmon fillets

Directions:
1. In a small bowl, mix together ingredients 1-7 to make the marinade.
2. Put salmon fillets in a large bowl and pour half the marinade over them. Coat well.
3. Pre-heat air fryer to 375 °F
4. Line air fryer basket with foil, and make some holes in the foil to match the air fryer basket holes (You could skip this step and just spray basket with cooking spray or use parchment paper liners with holes if you have them)
5. Transfer the salmon into the air fryer basket, making sure the fillets are not touching each other. Air fry for 8-10 minutes. Salmon is done when it flakes easily.
6. Meanwhile, pour the rest of the marinade into a small sauce pan and cook on stove over medium heat for a couple of minutes, until it thickens to form the glaze

7. When ready to serve, transfer salmon to plate and brush with glaze and sprinkle with chopped green onions and sesame seeds (optional).
8. Best served warm.

RECIPE NOTES

I cooked the salmon with the skin on. The skin comes off easily when cooked.

Cooking time may vary depending on the thickness of the salmon fillets and the brand of air fryer. Use an instant read thermometer inserted into the thickest side of the salmon to make sure it reaches an internal temperature of 140°F. Also, salmon flakes and separates from the skin easily when cooked.

If your air fryer is smaller, you will have to cook salmon in batches. Do not overcrowd the air fryer.

Goes well with air fried green beans, asparagus, baked potatoes or a green salad.

Keeps in the fridge for 3 days in an airtight container or wrapped tightly in plastic wrap.

To heat up, heat in a preheated air fryer at 375°F for 2 mins.

Salmon With Roasted Miso Vegetables

Servings: 2
Cooking Time: 10-30 Minutes

Ingredients:

- 300g/10½oz baby new potatoes, halved
- 150g/5½oz green beans, trimmed
- 150g/5½oz Tenderstem broccoli, sliced diagonally
- 2 tsp olive oil
- 2 x 150g/5½oz pieces skinless salmon fillets
- salt and freshly ground black pepper
- lemon wedges, to serve
- For the miso dressing
- 1 tbsp white miso
- 2 tsp olive oil
- 2 tsp white wine vinegar
- ½ tsp toasted sesame oil
- ½ tsp honey
- 1–2 tbsp hot water

Directions:

1. Preheat the oven to 230C/210C Fan/Gas 8 and put a roasting tin on the middle shelf to heat up.
2. Bring a pan of salted water to the boil and add the potatoes. Bring back up to the boil, cook for 6–7 minutes until tender, then drain and leave to steam dry for a couple of minutes.
3. Meanwhile, whisk the dressing ingredients together in a large bowl, adding a little hot water to thin the dressing to a pourable consistency.
4. Tip the potatoes, beans and broccoli into the preheated roasting tin, drizzle with oil and season with salt and pepper. Give everything a good mix, then roast for 10 minutes until the potatoes are soft and the vegetables are beginning to caramelise. Pour the dressing over and toss to coat.
5. Heat a non-stick frying pan over a high heat and season the salmon with a little salt and pepper. Lay the salmon in the pan and cook without moving for 3 minutes. Gently turn the fish over and cook for a further 2 minutes.
6. Serve the salmon with the vegetables and lemon wedges.

Recipe Tips

You can cook the potatoes and beans in an air fryer, set to 180C. When the par-boiled potatoes have steam-dried, toss them in some olive oil and add to the air fryer. Cook for 6–8 minutes, then add the beans and the broccoli. Cook for a further 3 minutes until the vegetables are crisped.

You can substitute ordinary broccoli and/or cauliflower, cut into florets, for the Tenderstem and beans.

Buttered Crab Rolls With Chive Mayo

Servings: 4

Ingredients:
- Chive Mayo
- 2 tablespoons mayonnaise
- 1 tablespoon fresh chives, minced
- ½ tablespoon olive oil
- 1 garlic clove, grated
- 1 teaspoon Worcestershire sauce
- ½ lemon, zested and juiced
- ¾ teaspoon kosher salt
- Crab Rolls
- 4 split-top hot dog buns
- 3 tablespoons unsalted butter, melted
- 12 ounces jumbo lump crab meat, cooked
- 1½ teaspoons Old Bay® seasoning
- 1 head butter lettuce, torn, for serving
- Lemon wedges, for serving

Directions:
1. Whisk all of the chive mayo ingredients together in a medium bowl, then set aside.
2. Brush the hot dog buns with the butter.
3. Place the crisper plate into the Smart Air Fryer basket.
4. Place the buns onto the crisper plate.
5. Adjust temperature to 415°F and time to 3 minutes, then press Start/Pause.
6. Remove the buns when done.
7. Mix the crab meat and Old Bay seasoning together, then add chive mayo to taste.
8. Lay lettuce in the bottom of each toasted hot dog bun, top with a generous mound of crab, then serve with lemon wedges on the side.

Air Fryer Fish Sticks

Servings: 4-6
Cooking Time: 20 Minutes

Ingredients:
- Nonstick olive oil spray
- 1 pound cod, sliced into 3-inch sticks
- 1/2 cup cornstarch
- 1/2 teaspoon kosher salt, plus more to taste
- 1/2 teaspoon black pepper
- 2 large eggs
- 1 cup panko breadcrumbs
- 1 teaspoon paprika
- For the pickle and caper tartar sauce
- 1/2 cup mayonnaise
- 1 tablespoon fresh lemon juice
- 1/4 cup minced pickles
- 2 tablespoons capers
- 1/8 teaspoon kosher salt
- To serve
- Chopped parsley or dill, optional

Directions:
1. Prep the air fryer:
2. Spray your air fryer pan with nonstick spray. Some people prefer to preheat their air fryer, but I think it's optional for this recipe.
3. Prepare the breading station:
4. Combine the cornstarch, salt, and pepper in a large shallow dish. In a separate shallow plate, whisk the eggs. Add panko and paprika to a third shallow dish.
5. Bread the fish:
6. Add fish sticks into the cornstarch and toss well to coat. Then add to egg mixture to coat and finally add to panko breadcrumbs making sure to coat all sides.
7. Air fry the fish sticks:
8. Working in batches, add fish sticks to your air fryer basket in an even layer. Spray them lightly with cooking spray.

9. Air fry for 6 minutes at 375°F. Flip fish sticks using tongs and air fry for another 4 to 6 minutes until golden brown. Season with salt to taste, if desired.
10. Repeat with second batch of fish sticks.
11. Simple Tip!
12. You can keep cooked fish sticks in a warm, 250°F oven, so they stay warm and crispy while you make the second batch.
13. Make the pickle and caper tartar sauce:
14. In a small bowl, combine mayonnaise, fresh lemon juice, minced pickles, capers, and kosher salt. Mix until well combined.
15. Serve:
16. Garnish with parsley or dill, if desired. Serve fish sticks with tartar sauce and lemon wedges.
17. Leftovers keep fine in the fridge for a few days in an airtight container. To reheat, air fry at 350°F for 3 minutes.

Fish Taco Bowl

Servings: 4
Cooking Time: 10 Minutes

Ingredients:

- 4 6 ounce boneless skinless fish fillets (such as blackfish, cod, mahi mahi, cut into 1 inch pieces)
- olive oil spray
- 2 to 3 teaspoons Cajun seasoning (or to taste)
- 1/4 cup mayonnaise
- 1 teaspoon sriracha (or chipotle en adobo sauce)
- 2 limes
- 5 cups slaw (red cabbage, white cabbage and shredded carrots)
- 1/2 tablespoon olive oil
- 1/2 teaspoon kosher salt
- cilantro (optional)

Directions:

1. Spritz fish all over with oil. Season all over with seasoning. Cut 1 lime into wedges and halve the other.
2. Combine mayo and sriracha or chipotle and squeeze 1/4 of the lime. Add a little water until it's easy to drizzle later.
3. Air fry the fish 6 minutes 400F shaking the basket half way.
4. Meanwhile, combine slaw with 1/2 tablespoon olive oil, remaining half lime and 1/2 teaspoon salt.
5. Divide on 4 plates, add fish on the side and drizzle the spicy mayo over the fish.
6. Serve with lime wedges and garnish with cilantro.
7. No air fryer, no problem! Heat a skillet on high heat, spray with oil and cook 5 to 6 minutes.

Air Fryer Tilapia

Servings: 2
Cooking Time: 6 Minutes

Ingredients:

- 2 Tilapia Filets about 6 ounces each
- 1 tablespoon olive oil
- 1 teaspoon chili powder
- 1/2 teaspoon paprika
- 1/2 teaspoon salt
- 1/4 teaspoon black pepper

Directions:

1. To make this air fryer fish recipe, begin by lightly rinsing and then pat each piece of fish dry with paper towels, then set aside.
2. In a small bowl, combine the chili powder, paprika, salt, and black pepper. Stir together to combine. Brush each filet with olive oil on both sides, or use olive oil spray, and then sprinkle to coat with seasoning mixture.
3. In a single layer, without overlapping, place tilapia in air fryer basket, without overlapping. Air Fry at cooking temperature of 350 degrees Fahrenheit, for 5-6 minutes, until golden brown.
4. Additional cook time may be needed as cooking times may vary depending on the thickness of fish.

NOTES

To confirm doneness, use a fork to flake tilapia fish fillet. It should flake easily.

Fish should be eaten with an internal temperature of 130-135 degrees F. Use a meat thermometer to confirm doneness.

I use fresh tilapia fillets for this simple recipe, but you can use frozen fillets as well. Add an additional 2-3 minutes to cooking process.

Air Fryer Scallops

Servings: 4
Cooking Time: 8 Minutes

Ingredients:

- 1 pound sea scallops
- 1 tablespoon unsalted butter melted, or olive oil
- 1 teaspoon minced garlic about 2 small cloves
- 1 teaspooon old bay seasoning
- 1/2 teaspoon kosher salt
- 1/4 teaspoon ground black pepper

Directions:

1. Remove any side muscle from the fresh scallops with a sharp knife. Rinse them under cold water and then pat dry with a paper towel.
2. Place scallops in a medium bowl, then add the butter, garlic, and seasonings. Toss together until the scallops are fully coated.
3. Spray basket with cooking spray or line with parchment paper. Then place the scallops in a single layer into the air fryer basket.
4. Air fry the scallops 400 degrees F for 8-10 minutes turning halfway through the cooking process, until scallops are tender and opaque.

NOTES

Optional Favorite Sauce: Extra butter sauce, cocktail sauce, herb garlic sauce, teriyaki sauce, chimichurri sauce, or fresh pesto sauce.

Optional Additional Toppings: Lemon wedge, fresh dill or parsley, roasted garlic, drizzle of chili oil or fresh thyme and mango salsa.

Air Fryer Spicy Shrimp Fajitas

Ingredients:

- 1 lb raw + Shelled Shrimp
- 1 large poblano chile
- 2 bell peppers
- 1/2 small yellow onion
- 1 jalapeno
- 2 cloves garlic - minced
- 2 tbs lime juice
- 4 tbs Fajita seasoning
- 4 tbs olive oil

Directions:

1. In a large bowl, combine all ingredients
2. Mix well
3. Toss everything in your air fryer
4. Cook at 370°F for 8 minutes
5. Remove basket and mix ingredients thoroughly
6. Return basket to air fryer and cook for another 4 minutes at 370°F
7. Add your favorite toppings and enjoy!

Crispy Coconut Shrimp

Servings: 4-5
Cooking Time: 20 Minutes

Ingredients:

- coconut shrimp:
- 1 ¼ pound jumbo raw shrimp (peeled + deveined)
- 1 cup EACH: shredded sweetened coconut AND Panko crumbs
- 1/3 cup all-purpose flour
- 2 large eggs
- ½ teaspoon EACH: garlic powder AND salt
- sweet and tangy sauce:
- 1/3 cup sweet chili sauce
- 2 teaspoons mayo
- ~ 1/2 lime, squeezed (more or less to taste)

Directions:

1. PREP: Rinse the shrimp under cold running water, then, pat them dry on paper towels. Set up a dredging station. The first bowl should contain the flour, garlic powder, and ½ teaspoon of salt (whisk to combine.) In the second bowl, add the two eggs and whisk to combine. The third bowl will contain

the shredded coconut and the Panko breadcrumbs, toss or stir to combine.

2. DREDGE: Grab the shrimp by the tail, dredge it in the flour, shake off any excess. Then, dip it in the egg mixture, and finally in the coconut mixture. Use your hands to press down so the crumbs adhere to the shrimp. Place the coated shrimp on a clean baking sheet. Continue with the remaining shrimp. At this point, you can freeze the shrimp for 30 minutes to make it easier to fry them or refrigerate until ready to fry. You can also fry or air fry them immediately.

3. COOK: FRY: Heat a large skillet over medium-high heat. Add a generous 1-1 ½ inches of oil tot he skillet and let it heat to about 350°F. Alternately, you could do this in a deep fryer set to 350°F. When heated, add a shrimp. Make sure the oil around the shrimp starts bubbling right away. Then, add 4-5 additional shrimp, make sure you do not overcrowd the pan. Cook for roughly 2 minutes per side (4-5 minutes total) or until the outside is golden brown and the shrimp curl up into a 'c' shape. Remove the shrimp with a slotted spoon and drain on a paper towel.

4. AIR FRYER: Preheat the air fryer according to manufacturers' directions at 375°F. Place the shrimp on a clean surface and spray the shrimp with coconut cooking spray (or any kind you like) place the sprayed side down in the air fryer and spray the other side with cooking spray. Cook the shrimp at 375°F for 6-8 minutes or until they cook all the way through, be sure to flip the shrimp around the halfway mark.

5. SAUCE: Combine the ingredients for the sauce in a bowl and whisk. You want to make sure to work the lumps out of the sauce completely. Taste and adjust with additional lime juice as desired. Serve with the shrimp!

Notes

If you're looking for a way to reheat the leftover coconut shrimp, I like to do so in an air fryer on the 'reheat' setting or in a traditional oven (at 400°F) for about 6-10 minutes.

SANDWICHES & BURGERS RECIPES

Air Fryer Black Bean Burger

Servings: 4
Cooking Time: 10 Minutes

Ingredients:
- Homemade Black Bean Burger
- 16 ounces black beans
- 1 egg
- 1/2 cup breadcrumbs
- 2 Tablespoons red onion chopped
- 1 Tablespoon bell pepper green
- 1 teaspoon chili powder
- 1/4 teaspoon salt
- 1/4 teaspoon ground black pepper
- Frozen Black Bean Burger
- 4 black bean burger patties
- Mashed Avocado Topping
- 1 medium avocado
- 1/2 teaspoon chili powder
- 1/4 teaspoon salt
- 1/4 teaspoon pepper
- Optional Toppings
- 2 slices tomato
- lettuce
- 2 slices cheese American
- 2 slices onion

Directions:
1. Homemade Black Bean Burger Recipe
2. Mash the black beans in a bowl with a fork or potato masher.
3. Add the onion and pepper to a food processor and pulse until mixed.
4. Add the vegetables to a large bowl with the black beans and stir until combined. Stir in the breadcrumbs until combined.
5. In a separate bowl add the egg and seasonings and whisk together. Add in the black bean mixture.
6. Evenly create 4 black bean burgers with the mixture.
7. Place the uncooked patties in the basket of the air fryer and spray the tops with olive oil. Air fry at 380 degrees Fahrenheit for 10 minutes of cooking time, flipping the patties halfway through the cooking process.
8. Serve with optional mashed avocado mixture and your favorite toppings.
9. Frozen Black bean Burger
10. Place the frozen black bean patties in a single layer in the air fryer basket.
11. Air fry the black bean burgers at 380 degrees Fahrenheit for 10 minutes, flipping the black bean patties halfway through the cook time.
12. Optional Mashed Avocado Topping
13. Mash the avocado in a small bowl.
14. Add the salt pepper, and chili powder into the mashed avocado. Mix well.
15. Remove the cooked black bean burgers from the air fryer and top with the avocado mixture and any additional toppings before serving.

NOTES

Cook black bean burgers in the air fryer for 10 minutes, flipping the burgers halfway through the cooking process. Add an additional minute or two of cook time if needed.

Use traditional toppings such as tomato slices, lettuce, red onion, and cheese. You can also top it with Worcestershire sauce or even diced green chilis to spice it up.

Air Fried Black Bean Burger

Ingredients:
- 2 cans of seasoned black beans
- 1 cup of seasoned breadcrumbs (can substitute with quinoa)
- ¼ cup of grated white onion
- 1 whole egg
- ½ tsp chili powder
- Salt and pepper
- Hot sauce
- Swiss cheese (optional)
- Hamburger buns (can substitute with lettuce and make lettuce wrapped burgers)
- Mayonnaise (can substitute with light mayo, avocado mayo, etc.)
- Lettuce
- Tomato, sliced

Directions:
1. Use cheese grater to grate a quarter of an onion.
2. In a bowl, mash 2 cans of drained black beans. Beans don't have to be completely mashed. The texture is up to you.
3. In the same bowl, add 1 egg, onion shavings, breadcrumbs, chili powder, salt and pepper. We added a dash of hot sauce as well.
4. Mash to combine. It might be easier to use hands.
5. Shape into patties.
6. Place parchment paper in air fryer basket. If you do not have parchment paper, it's okay! You can go ahead to step 7.
7. Place 1 or 2 patties into the air fryer basket and brush one side with olive oil.
8. Set air fryer at 350 F for 5 minutes.
9. Once the 5 minutes are done, take out and flip the patties over. Put back in air fryer and cook for 3 more minutes at the same temperature.
10. Optional: if you'd like to add cheese. Place one slice over the patty and cook at 300 F for 1 minute to melt the cheese.
11. Build your burger with these delicious black bean patties and enjoy!

Air Fryer Turkey Burgers

Servings: 4
Cooking Time: 17 Minutes

Ingredients:
- 1 pound ground turkey not extra lean
- 1 tablespoon olive oil
- 1 egg yolk
- 2 tablespoons seasoned bread crumbs
- 1 teaspoon soy sauce
- ½ teaspoon onion powder
- ¼ teaspoon garlic powder
- salt & pepper
- ¼ cup barbecue sauce optional
- For Serving
- hamburger buns
- lettuce tomato, onion

Directions:
1. Gently combine all ingredients in a bowl.
2. Form into 4 patties, ½" thick. Using your thumb, create a small indent in the patties. Refrigerate 30 minutes
3. Preheat air fryer to 350°F.
4. Brush patties with barbecue sauce if using and place in a single layer in the air fryer basket. Cook 6 minutes. Flip over and cook an additional 6-8 minutes or until cooked through (165°F).
5. Serve on buns with desired toppings.

Notes

Poultry must reach 165°F to be safely cooked.

Chilling the burgers first helps them hold their shape and allows the flavors to blend. If you're in a real rush you can skip this step but be gentle when flipping them. If you only can get 'extra lean' turkey or chicken, add a little bit of fat for best results. A tablespoon of olive oil or some finely chopped bacon are favorites in our regular turkey burgers.

Most importantly do not overcook. I recommend an instant read thermometer! Meat is expensive and this is a minimal investment that ensures the best cook.

Air Fryer Hamburgers

Servings: 4

Cooking Time: 10 Minutes

Ingredients:

- 1 pound 80% lean ground beef
- 2 tablespoons melted butter
- 1 tablespoon beef base (such as Better than Bouillon®)
- freshly ground black pepper to taste

Directions:

1. Preheat an air fryer to 400 degrees F (195 degrees C).
2. Form beef into 4 patties, approximately 3/4 inches thick and 4 1/2 inches in diameter. Make the patties slightly bigger than the buns to allow for shrinkage.
3. Whisk together warm melted butter and beef soup base in a small bowl. Brush lightly onto both sides of patties and season with pepper. Set patties into the air fryer basket. Depending on the size of your air fryer, you may need to cook them in batches.
4. Air-fry patties for 7 minutes, flipping halfway through, for medium doneness. For well done, air-fry for an additional 2 minutes.

Cook's Notes:

This recipe was developed using a 2.8-quart basket-style air fryer. Results will vary depending on air fryer size and brand, and thickness of your patties. You may need to adjust cook time to achieve your preferred degree of doneness.

If excessive smoking occurs, add water to bottom of air fryer to help prevent dripping grease from burning.

Air Fryer Grilled Cheese Sandwich

Servings: 1

Cooking Time: 5 Minutes

Ingredients:

- 2 slices bread
- 1 teaspoon butter
- 2 slices cheddar cheese
- 2 slices turkey (optional)

Directions:

1. Preheat the air fryer to 350 degrees.
2. Spread the butter on one side of the bread. Add cheese, turkey if using and cover with another piece of bread, buttered on the opposite side.
3. Place the sandwich inside the Air Fryer. Set the time for 5 minutes. Turn half way.
4. The grilled cheese sandwich suppose to look like on the picture, toasty and with lots of melted cheese!

Notes

Use a toothpick to prevent the top bread slice from frying around. In some air fryers its not needed.

You don't need to pretoast the bread. Cook all at once. Enjoy immediately after cooking, while hot and crunchy. To reheat just pop into the air fryer for couple minutes at 400 degrees.

My favorite cheese to use in the air fryer grilled cheese sandwich in sharp cheddar. It melts lovely and looks beautiful.

Cuban Sandwiches

Servings: 2

Ingredients:
- Roasted Pork Tenderloin
- 1 pork tenderloin
- 1 orange, zested and juiced
- 1 lime, zested and juiced
- 1 tablespoon olive oil
- 1 tablespoon brown sugar
- 2 garlic cloves, grated
- 2 teaspoons smoked paprika
- 1 teaspoon ground cumin
- 2 teaspoons kosher salt
- Sandwiches
- 2 Cuban sandwich rolls (8-inch length), halved lengthwise
- 1½ tablespoons unsalted butter, melted
- Yellow mustard, as needed
- 5 ounces ham, thinly sliced
- Dill pickle slices, as needed
- 4 Swiss cheese slices
- Items Needed
- Meat tenderizer

Directions:
1. Place the pork tenderloin on a cutting board. Carefully cut down the center lengthwise with a knife, not cutting all the way through, opening it up like a book.
2. Continue making small cuts into the thickest part of the meat to open it up until it is roughly rectangular in shape.
3. Lay the pork between 2 pieces of plastic wrap, then pound it to ½-inch thickness using a meat tenderizer.
4. Combine the orange zest and juice, lime zest and juice, olive oil, brown sugar, grated garlic, paprika, cumin, and kosher salt in a large resealable plastic bag.
5. Add the pork tenderloin and shake to mix everything together. Marinate at room temperature for 40 minutes.
6. Place the crisper plate into the Smart Air Fryer basket.
7. Select the Preheat function, then press Start/Pause.
8. Remove the pork from the marinade and place it onto the preheated crisper plate.
9. Set temperature to 425°F and time to 15 minutes, press Shake, then press Start/Pause.
10. Flip the pork tenderloin halfway through cooking. The Shake Reminder will let you know when.
11. Remove the pork tenderloin when done and let rest for 10 minutes before slicing into strips.
12. Brush the inside of each Cuban roll with melted butter, then spread with the yellow mustard.
13. Layer the pork tenderloin slices, ham, and dill pickle slices on of one side of each roll, top with 2 slices of the Swiss cheese, then place the other side of the roll on top.
14. Place the sandwiches onto the crisper plate.
15. Set temperature to 425°F and time to 3 minutes, then press Start/Pause.
16. Remove the sandwiches when done, halve them crosswise, then serve.

Air Fryer Copycat Chick Fil A Sandwich

Servings: 2

Cooking Time: 15 Minutes

Ingredients:
- 2 medium eggs
- 1 cup milk whole
- 2 chicken breasts boneless, skinless
- 1 cup all purpose flour
- 1 cup breadcrumbs plain
- 1/2 cup pickle juice
- 2 Tablespoons powdered sugar
- 1 teaspoon kosher salt
- 1/4 teaspoon paprika
- 1/4 teaspoom chili powder

- 1/2 teaspoon white pepper black pepper can be substituted

Directions:
1. Presoak the chicken breasts in pickle juice in a medium size bowl for 20 minutes.
2. Place chicken breasts into a sealable bag and pound the chicken breasts to about ½-inch thickness with a meat mallet.
3. Then cut the chicken breasts in half to make 4 total pieces of chicken.
4. Whisk milk and eggs together in a shallow bowl then place the chicken breasts into the milk mixture and allow them to sit for 30 minutes.
5. In a separate bowl mix the breadcrumbs, flour, powdered sugar, salt, paprika, pepper and chili powder together.
6. Preheat the air fryer to 400 degrees F for 5 minutes.
7. Remove the chicken breasts from the egg mixture and dip chicken pieces in the seasoned flour mixture. Shake each piece gently to remove excess flour.
8. Place each piece on a baking sheet until you are ready to begin to air fry.
9. Place the chicken breasts into the air fryer basket. Spray the tops of the chicken with olive oil spray or avocado oil spray.
10. Air fry the chicken at 400 degrees F for 17-19 minutes, flip chicken halfway through the cooking process and spray the tops to get extra crispy chicken.
11. Use an instant-read meat thermometer to make sure the internal temperature has reached 165 degrees F.
12. Serve on brioche buns with favorite sandwich fixings.

NOTES

Optional Favorite Dipping Sauce: Ranch dressing, honey mustard sauce, spicy mayonnaise or homemade chick fil a sauce.

Optional Additional Toppings: Hot sauce, slice of cheese, shredded lettuce, Dijon or yellow mustard, sliced tomato or dill pickle slices.

Optional Additional Flavors: Black pepper, garlic powder, teaspoon lemon juice and cayenne pepper.

I make this recipe in my Cosori 5.8 qt. air fryer or 6.8 quart air fryer. Depending on your air fryer, size and wattages, cooking time may need to be adjusted 1-2 minutes.

Grilled Ham & Cheese Sandwiches

Servings: 2

Ingredients:
- 2 tablespoons (30 grams) mayonnaise, divided
- 4 slices rustic cracked sourdough bread, about ½-inch (13-millimetres) thick
- 4 slices of sharp cheddar cheese
- 6 slices of tomatoes, optional
- 6 slices deli-sliced black forest ham
- 4 slices provolone cheese

Directions:
1. Spread the mayonnaise on both sides of each slice of bread.
2. Assemble the sandwich by taking one slice of bread and layering 2 slices of cheddar, 3 slices of tomato, 3 slices of ham, 2 slices of provolone, and the other slice of sourdough on top. Repeat for the second sandwich.
3. Place the cooking pot into the base of the Smart Indoor Grill, followed by the grill grate.
4. Select the Air Grill function on low heat, adjust temperature to 425°F (215°C) and time to 6 minutes, press Shake, then press Start/Pause to preheat.
5. Place the sandwiches onto the preheated grill grate, gently press down on each sandwich using a spatula, then close the lid.
6. Flip the sandwiches halfway through cooking and gently press down again on each sandwich using a spatula. The Shake Reminder will let you know when.
7. Remove the sandwiches when done and let cool for 2 minutes before slicing in half diagonally.
8. Serve immediately.

Air Fryer Loose Meat Sandwiches

Servings: 6

Cooking Time: 15 Minutes

Ingredients:
- 1 pound ground beef
- 1 teaspoon olive oil
- ½ yellow onion diced
- 1 clove garlic minced
- 2 tablespoons Worcestershire sauce
- ¼ cup yellow mustard
- ⅓ cup Kosher dill pickles sliced
- salt and pepper to taste
- Bread or rolls - your choice!

Directions:
1. Preheat the Air Fryer 375°F.
2. Add onion and ground beef to a glass dish that will fit in your Air Fryer. Put in the Air Fryer.
3. Cook for 5 minutes and then carefully pull out the rack and use a spatula to break up the ground beef. Add garlic, Worcestershire, and mustard. Stir until combined, and cook for another 5 minutes or until the meat is no longer pink. Remove and set aside.
4. Add two pieces of toast to the Air Fryer and toast for 3 minutes - flip halfway through.
5. Pile meat onto the roll or bread, top with pickles, and cover. Repeat until you have four sandwiches.

Minted Lamb Burgers

Servings: 4

Cooking Time: 15 Minutes

Ingredients:
- 500g lamb leg steaks
- 4 x Specially Selected seeded burger buns
- 1 x tsp dried mixed herbs
- 70g mayonnaise
- 1 x tsp mint sauce
- Half iceberg lettuce
- 4 x salad tomatoes
- 1 x red onion
- Sea salt and black pepper

Directions:
1. Chop the lamb into small chunks.
2. Put into a food processor, add the mixed herbs, season with salt and pepper and process till the lamb is minced.
3. Divide into four.
4. Roll into a ball and then flatter into 4 patties.
5. Preheat the airfryer to 180°C.
6. Put the burgers onto the fry tray.
7. Close the fry basket and cook for 15 mins.
8. Toast the cut sides of the buns.
9. Mix the mint sauce with the mayo.
10. Top the bun bases with lettuce, sliced tomato and red onion.
11. Top with a burger, drizzle over the minted mayo – top with the bun lid and serve.

BEEF, PORK & LAMB RECIPES

Air Fryer Steak With Garlic-herb Butter

Servings: 2

Ingredients:
- Deselect All
- One 1-pound sirloin steak, about 1 inch thick
- Kosher salt and freshly ground black pepper
- 4 tablespoons unsalted butter, at room temperature
- 1 tablespoon finely chopped fresh parsley
- 1 tablespoon finely chopped fresh chives
- 1 small clove garlic, finely grated
- 1/4 teaspoon crushed red pepper flakes

Directions:
1. Allow the steak to sit at room temperature for 30 minutes before cooking.
2. Preheat a 3.5-quart air fryer to 400 degrees F. Season the steak on both sides with a generous pinch of salt and several grinds of black pepper. Place the steak in the center of the air fryer basket and cook until desired doneness, about 10 minutes for medium-rare, 12 minutes for medium and 14 minutes for medium-well. Transfer the steak to a cutting board and allow to rest, about 10 minutes.
3. Meanwhile, mash together the butter, parsley, chives, garlic and crushed red pepper in a small bowl until combined. Slice the steak against the grain into 1/4-inch-thick pieces. Top with the garlic-herb butter.

Air Fryer Ham And Cheese Turnovers

Servings: 4
Cooking Time: 10 Minutes

Ingredients:
- 1 tube (13.8 ounces) refrigerated pizza crust
- 1/4 pound thinly sliced black forest deli ham
- 1 medium pear, thinly sliced and divided
- 1/4 cup chopped walnuts, toasted
- 2 tablespoons crumbled blue cheese

Directions:
1. Preheat air fryer to 400. On a lightly floured surface, unroll pizza crust into a 12-in. square. Cut into 4 squares. Layer ham, half of pear slices, walnuts and blue cheese diagonally over half of each square to within 1/2 in. of edges. Fold 1 corner over filling to the opposite corner, forming a triangle; press edges with a fork to seal.
2. In batches, arrange turnovers in a single layer on greased tray in air-fryer basket; spritz with cooking spray. Cook until golden brown, 4-6 minutes on each side. Garnish with remaining pear slices.

Air-fryer Pigs In Blankets

Servings: 4
Cooking Time: 10-12 Minutes

Ingredients:
- 8 rashers smoked or unsmoked streaky bacon
- 8 pork chipolatas

Directions:
1. Wrap one rasher of bacon around each chipolata, then arrange in a single layer in the air-fryer basket.
2. Cook at 180C for 10-12 mins until the bacon and chipolatas are cooked through. If you prefer your bacon extra-crisp, cook for a few minutes more, but keep a close eye on the sausages.

Juicy Lucy Sliders

Servings: 6
Cooking Time: 14 Minutes

Ingredients:
- Burger Patties:
- 1 pound ground beef
- 1½ teaspoons kosher salt
- 1 tablespoon ground black pepper
- 1 tablespoon onion powder
- 6 slices American cheese
- Oil spray
- For Serving:
- 6 slider buns, sliced in half & toasted
- Ketchup
- Mustard
- Mayonnaise
- Lettuce
- Tomato
- Onion

Directions:
1. Combine the ground beef, salt, pepper, and onion powder in a large bowl.
2. Divide the meat into 6 equal portions.
3. Form a patty with each portion, then press the cheese into the center of each until the cheese is completely enclosed by the meat. Set aside.
4. Select the Preheat function on the Air Fryer, adjust temperature to 380°F, then press Start/Pause.
5. Spray the preheated air fryer basket with oil spray.
6. Place the burger patties into the preheated air fryer.
7. Set temperature to 380°F and time to 14 minutes, press Shake, then press Start/Pause.
8. Flip the burger patties halfway through cooking. The Shake Reminder will let you know when.
9. Remove the burger patties when done and let rest for 5 minutes.
10. Assemble the burgers with toasted buns, ketchup, mustard, mayonnaise, lettuce, tomato, and onion.
11. Serve the sliders warm.

Air Fryer Top Round Roast

Servings: 4
Cooking Time: 48 Minutes

Ingredients:
- 3 pound Beef Top Round Roast
- 1/2 teaspoon salt
- 1/4 teaspoon pepper
- 1/4 cup beef broth
- 16 ounces mini potatoes
- 16 ounces baby carrots

Directions:
1. Prepare the roast, by lightly coating it with olive oil, and sprinkling the salt and pepper to coat both sides.
2. Preheat the oven to 400 degrees Fahrenheit.
3. Place the roast in the basket, and cook at 400 degrees. Cook for 25-28 minutes.
4. While the roast is cooking, toss the carrots and potatoes in olive oil, salt and pepper. Let sit until the top of the roast is done cooking.
5. Once the roast has cooked the first 25-28 minutes, turn the roast over, baste with the beef broth, and add the prepared the carrots and potatoes. Return basket to air fryer and cook at 400 degrees for an additional 18-20 minutes.
6. Potatoes and carrots should be soft, and the internal temperature of the roast is 145 degrees. Allow the roast to rest for 5-10 minutes before serving.

NOTES

This roast can be sliced and served for dinner, or thinly sliced for roast beef sandwich meat. My roast, was three pounds, and was rolled and tied with string. After cooking for about 28 minutes, I turned the roast over, and it opened to be a less thick.

If you keep your roast tied together, it may take a few extra minutes to cook in the center, so be sure to get internal temperature to 145 degrees.

If meat finishes before the potatoes and carrots are softened to your liking, remove the meat to let it rest, and continue cooking the potatoes and carrots for an additional 5 minutes, or until they reach your preferred doneness.

Peppercorn Steak Recipe

Ingredients:
- 200g sirloin steak
- 50g unsalted butter
- 2 shallots, finely diced
- 100ml beef stock
- 2 tbsp Worcestershire Sauce
- 2 tbsp brandy
- 2 tbsp double cream
- 1 tbsp Dijon mustard
- 1 tbsp olive oil
- 1 tbsp green peppercorns
- Black and white peppercorns, to taste

Directions:
1. Dry the steaks with kitchen roll and press the black and white peppercorns into both sides, then cover the steaks with foil and refrigerate for 2-3 hours.
2. Place the steak in a 180°C air fryer and cook for approximately 6 minutes for rare, 8 for medium, and 10 for well done, turning the steak halfway through to caramelise both sides.
3. Make the sauce by heating up the oil and butter in a large frying pan and cooking the shallots over medium heat until soft. Then add the Worcestershire sauce, brandy, and stock to the frying pan.
4. Cook this rapidly, scraping the bottom of the frying pan to incorporate the flavour, then add the green peppercorns, mustard, and cream, then season to taste.
5. Remove the meat from the air fryer and leave to rest for approximately 5 minutes, then slice and add to the sauce and stir to combine the flavours.
6. Top tip! Serve with thick cut chips, wedges, salad, fluffy rice or tender vegetables for a delicious meal.

Air-fryer Rosemary Sausage Meatballs

Servings: 2
Cooking Time: 10 Minutes

Ingredients:
- 2 tablespoons olive oil
- 4 garlic cloves, minced
- 1 teaspoon curry powder
- 1 large egg, lightly beaten
- 1 jar (4 ounces) diced pimientos, drained
- 1/4 cup dry bread crumbs
- 1/4 cup minced fresh parsley
- 1 tablespoon minced fresh rosemary
- 2 pounds bulk pork sausage
- Pretzel sticks, optional

Directions:
1. Preheat air fryer to 400. In a small skillet, heat oil over medium heat; saute garlic with curry powder until tender, 1-2 minutes. Cool slightly.
2. In a bowl, combine egg, pimientos, bread crumbs, parsley, rosemary and garlic mixture. Add sausage; mix lightly but thoroughly.
3. Shape into 1-1/4-in. balls. Place in a single layer on tray in air-fryer basket; cook until lightly browned and cooked through, 7-10 minutes. If desired, serve with pretzels.

Air-fryer Flank Steak And Fennel

Servings: 4
Cooking Time: 18 Minutes

Ingredients:
- ¼ cup olive oil
- 2 teaspoon lemon zest
- 1 teaspoon salt
- ¼ teaspoon black pepper
- 14 - 16 ounce beef flank steak, trimmed to an even thickness
- 12 ounce tiny red new potatoes, quartered
- 1 cup quartered, cored, and sliced fennel

Directions:

1. Preheat air fryer at 375°F. In a large bowl combine oil, lemon zest, salt, and pepper. Remove half of the oil mixture and rub over meat. Add potatoes and fennel to remaining oil mixture; toss to coat.
2. Spread potato mixture in air-fryer basket. Top with meat. Cook 18 to 20 minutes or until meat registers 135°F to 145°F and potatoes are tender, turning meat and rearranging potato mixture once. Transfer meat to a plate; cover and let stand 5 minutes. Thinly slice meat across the grain and serve with potato mixture.

Reheat Steak In Air Fryer

Servings: 2
Cooking Time: 8 Minutes
Ingredients:
- 1 pound steak previously cooked

Directions:
1. Preheat the air fryer to 350 degrees Fahrenheit.
2. Add the steak in a single layer to the air fryer basket and air fry for 6-8 minutes, flipping the steak halfway through cooking time.
3. Remove the steak from the air fryer and cover it for a few minutes with aluminum foil before serving.
4. Serve with a dollop of butter and your favorite sides.

NOTES

If the steak is not reheated enough to your liking, add 2-3 minutes of cooking time at 320 degrees Fahrenheit to the reheating process. The lower temperature will ensure you're not overcooking the steak.

Serve your favorite side dishes such as baked potatoes, sweet potatoes, or green beans with reheated steak.

Air Fryer "shake 'n Bake" Style Pork Chops

Servings: 3
Cooking Time: 12 Minutes
Ingredients:
- 3 (6oz.) ((170g)) pork chops, rinsed & patted dry
- Ice water, beaten egg, milk, or mayo, to moisten the pork
- Shake 'n Bake Style Seasoned Coating Mix
- Oil spray, to coat the pork chops
- Air Fryer Parchment Paper (optional)

Directions:
1. Preheat Air Fryer at 380°F/195°C for 4 minutes.
2. Moisten the pork chops based on seasoned coating mix instructions (or by using ice water, beaten egg, milk, or mayo). Coat with the seasoned coating mix.
3. Spray air fryer basket/tray with oil or place a perforated parchment sheet in the air fryer basket/tray & lightly coat with oil spray (this helps keep the pork chops coating from sticking and coming off).
4. Place the coated pork chops in a single layer (cook in batches if needed). Make sure pork chops are not touching or the coating may flake off when you flip them. Lightly coat the pork chops with oil spray.
5. Air Fry at 380°F/195°C for about 8-12 minutes. After 6 minutes of cooking, flip the pork chops and then continue cooking for the remainder of time or until golden and internal temperature reaches 145-160°F, depending on your doneness preference.

Air Fryer Flank Steak

Servings: 6
Cooking Time: 15 Minutes

Ingredients:

- 2 pounds flank steak
- Kosher salt, to taste
- Black pepper, to taste
- 1 cup dry red wine
- 2 tablespoons olive oil
- 2 tablespoons Worcestershire sauce
- 3 cloves garlic, minced
- 1 teaspoon Dijon mustard
- ½ teaspoon dried rosemary
- SAUCE:
- 1 cup beef broth
- 2 tablespoons butter

Directions:

1. Using a knife, score the steak on both sides with shallow cuts across the grain in a criss-cross pattern. Season both sides with salt and black pepper.
2. In a 2-cup measuring cup, whisk together the red wine, olive oil, Worcestershire sauce, garlic, Dijon, and rosemary. Pour the mixture into a plastic zipper bag, then place the steak in the bag and massage the marinade into the meat. Refrigerate for 4-8 hours.
3. Remove the steak from the bag and place it on a cutting board, then pour the marinade in a saucepan and set it aside.
4. Pat the steak dry with paper towels. Let it rest and come to room temperature for 30 minutes.
5. Preheat the air fryer to 400 degrees F. Place the steak inside, and cook for 5-7 minutes on each side, flipping once. (5 mins each side for 130 degrees/med-rare)
6. Remove the steak and allow it to rest on a cutting board for 10 minutes, then slice thinly against the grain.
7. While the steak rests, make the sauce (optional). Add beef broth to the saucepan with the marinade. Bring it to a boil over medium-high heat, then reduce the heat and simmer until the sauce thickens. Stir in the butter, taste, and season if necessary.

NOTES

HOW TO COOK FROZEN FLANK STEAK IN THE AIR FRYER:

Prepare the recipe through step 3, discarding the marinade, patting the steak dry, and placing the steak back in the zipper bag. Freeze it until ready to cook.

When ready to cook, preheat the air fryer to 400 degrees F. Spray the fryer basket with cooking spray, place the steak inside, and cook for 10-15 minutes on each side, flipping once, until the thickest part of the meat reads 130-165 degrees F (based on your desired doneness) on a meat thermometer.

Remove the steak and allow it to rest on a cutting board for 10 minutes, then slice thinly against the grain.

HOW TO REHEAT FLANK STEAK IN THE AIR FRYER:

Preheat the air fryer to 400 degrees F. Spray the fryer basket with cooking spray, place the steak inside, and cook for 5-7 minutes until warmed through.

Remove the steak and allow it to rest on a cutting board for 10 minutes, then slice thinly against the grain.

Air Fryer Roast Beef

Servings: 7
Cooking Time: 35 Minutes

Ingredients:

- 2 lb beef roast top round or eye of round is best
- oil for spraying
- Rub
- 1 tbs kosher salt
- 1 tsp black pepper
- 2 tsp garlic powder
- 1 tsp summer savory OR thyme

Directions:

1. Mix all rub ingredients and rub into roast.

2. Place fat side down in the basket of the air fryer (or set up for rotisserie if your air fryer is so equipped)
3. Lightly spray with oil.
4. Set fryer to 400 degrees F and air fry for 20 minutes; turn fat-side up and spray lightly with oil. Continue cooking for 15 additional minutes at 400 degrees F.
5. Remove the roast from the fryer, tent with foil and let the meat rest for 10 minutes.
6. The time given should produce a rare roast which should be 125 degrees F on a meat thermometer. Additional time will be needed for medium, medium-well and well. Always use a meat thermometer to test the temperature.
7. Approximate times for medium and well respectively are 40 minutes and 45 minutes. Remember to always use a meat thermometer as times are approximate and fryers differ by wattage.

Air Fryer Meatloaf

Servings: 4
Cooking Time: 25 Minutes

Ingredients:

- 1 pound lean ground beef
- ½ green bell pepper finely diced
- ⅓ cup seasoned bread crumbs
- ¼ cup onion* finely diced, see note
- 2 tablespoons milk
- 2 tablespoons parmesan cheese grated
- 1 tablespoon fresh parsley chopped
- 1 clove garlic minced
- 1 egg yolk
- ½ teaspoon Italian seasoning
- ¼ teaspoon salt and pepper to taste
- Topping
- ¼ cup tomato sauce
- ¼ cup chili sauce

Directions:

1. Preheat air fryer to 350°F.
2. Mix all meatloaf ingredients in a large bowl just until combined.
3. Divide the mixture into 2 and shape into small meatloaves, about 5" long by 2" wide.
4. Cook in the air fryer for 20 minutes.
5. Combine topping ingredients in a small bowl. Add topping and cook an additional 5-7 minutes or until meatloaf reaches 165°F.
6. Rest 5 minutes before serving.

Notes

For a milder onion flavor, fry the onion in 1 tablespoon butter until tender. Cool completely before adding.
Don't overmix the meat, mix just until combined.
Preheat the air fryer before adding the meatloaf.
Air Fryers can vary so be sure to use an instant read thermometer to check the internal temperature of the meatloaf and ensure it reaches 165° F.
Check the meatloaf early to ensure it doesn't overcook. Add more time as needed.
Rest the meatloaf before slicing so it doesn't fall apart.

Bacon Wrapped Brussels Sprouts

Servings: 18
Cooking Time: 25 Minutes

Ingredients:

- 1 package (9 slices) bacon strips
- 18 brussels sprouts
- 2 tablespoons maple syrup
- 1/2 teaspoon ground black pepper (or to taste)

Directions:

1. Preheat oven to 375F.
2. Cut each bacon strip in half crosswise (about 5-inches long). Wrap each strip around each brussels sprout. Secure each wrapped brussels sprout with a toothpick and place on a parchment-lined quarter sheet baking pan.
3. Brush the wrapped brussels sprouts with maple syrup and sprinkle with black pepper to taste. Bake until crispy to your desired level of crispiness, about 25-30 minutes.
4. Serve immediately.

NOTES

Wrapping the bacon: How you wrap your bacon will determine how it cooks. If you like crispy bacon, wrap loosely, leaving some space between the strips as you go around. If you prefer chewier bacon, wrap tightly and overlap a little.

Air fryer instructions: Place the wrapped brussels sprouts in the air fryer basket in a single layer. Cook at 375F for 13-15 minutes until the bacon is browned and crispy.

How to store: Store leftover bacon wrapped brussels sprouts in the refrigerator for up to three days. Before placing in an airtight container, allow the brussels sprouts to cool to room temperature. This will ensure they don't get soggy.

How to reheat: Reheat in a 350 F preheated oven for 10-15 minutes until warm and crispy. You can also reheat in the air fryer at 350F for 5-10 minutes until warmed through.

Air Fryer Copycat Taco Bell Crunchwrap

Ingredients:

- 10 inch flour tortillas
- Ground beef
- Shredded lettuce
- Cherry tomatoes quartered, or diced regular tomatoes
- Sour cream
- Mexican cheese blend, shredded
- Tortilla chips

Directions:

1. Pre-cook the ground beef using the spices of your choice and set aside.
2. Make the wrap by laying the tortilla down on a cutting board. Cut a line from the center of the tortilla to the bottom edge.
3. Starting at the bottom left quarter, add sour cream and tortilla chips. To the top left quarter, add the lettuce and tomatoes. On the top right quarter, sprinkle on some cheese. Finally, on the last quarter, sprinkle on the ground beef.
4. Starting with the bottom left corner and fold it up over the top left. Then fold it over to the top right. Finally, fold it down to the bottom right.
5. Cook at 370F for about 6 minutes, or until the tortilla is crispy and the cheese is melted. We recommend flipping over halfway so an even, crispy result.
6. Serve with any dipping sauce or salsa and enjoy!
7. Pro Tip: fill these wraps with as much or as little toppings as you want. Measure with your

Air Fryer Brown Sugar Bacon Crackers

Servings: 2
Cooking Time: 5 Minutes

Ingredients:

- 8 crackers flax seed or multigrain
- 3-4 strips bacon
- 2 tablespoons brown sugar

Directions:

1. Preheat the air fryer to 400°F.
2. Cut your bacon slightly larger than your cracker. Cook the bacon for 4 minutes in the air fryer.
3. Place the crackers in the air fryer basket, stack bacon on top, and sprinkle with brown sugar
4. Cook for 1-2 minutes until golden brown.

Air Fryer Bacon

Servings: 5
Cooking Time: 10 Minutes

Ingredients:

- 10 slices bacon thinly sliced

Directions:

1. Preheat the Air Fryer to 400 degrees Fahrenheit.
2. Place the bacon slices in the basket of the air fryer in a single layer. (It's ok if the bacon overlaps a little)
3. Close the basket door and cook at 400 degrees Fahrenheit (205 degrees Celcius) for 10 minutes.

4. Check the bacon after 10 minutes for crispiness. If you would like the bacon to be crispier, add another minute or two of cook time.
5. Remove to a plate and blot with paper towels to soak up any excess grease before serving.

NOTES

I use a Cosori 5.8 and this is the perfect time and temp for this Air Fryer. All Air Fryers cook differently and have different power wattages, so you may have to adjust the time for this recipe if using a different Air Fryer. It's always best to consult the book that came with your brand of Air Fryer before trying a new recipe.

EXPERT TIPS AND FAQS:

HOW DO I KEEP BACON FROM SMOKING IN THE AIR FRYER?

Almost all Air Fryers will smoke when cooking bacon. To cut down on the smoke, add a ½ cup of water to the basket bottom of the air fryer before cooking. You can also add a piece of bread to the bottom of the basket to catch the grease as the bacon is cooking, which will also reduce the smoke.

HOW LONG DO I COOK THICK BACON IN THE AIR FRYER?

I love my thick-cut bacon, and if I am cooking it in the Air Fryer it will take longer than 10 minutes. I cook thick-cut bacon in my Air Fryer for 14-15 minutes until it is perfectly crispy. I'll also twist the bacon to make thick bacon sticks to snack on. You can find the twisted bacon recipe here.

HOW LONG DO I COOK BACON IN THE AIR FRYER?

The cook time for bacon will depend on the type of bacon as well as the thickness of the bacon. Thinly sliced bacon: I cook perfectly crispy bacon in the Air Fryer at 10-12 minutes. (Closer to 10 minutes if I am only making a few pieces, closer to 12 minutes if I am filling up the basket.) Thick sliced bacon: For thicker bacon, I add a few minutes and cook between 14-15 minutes.

Air Fryer Bacon Wrapped Brussels Sprouts

Servings: 4
Cooking Time: 10 Minutes

Ingredients:

- 12 Brussels sprouts, trimmed and halved
- 2 teaspoons Montreal steak seasoning
- 12 slices bacon, cut in half widthwise

Directions:

1. Preheat the air fryer to 400 degrees F (200 degrees C).
2. Place halved Brussels sprouts in a bowl; sprinkle with steak seasoning and toss to coat.
3. Wrap a half slice of bacon around a Brussels sprout half and place seam-side-down in the basket of the air fryer. Repeat with remaining bacon and Brussels sprouts.
4. Cook for 10 minutes undisturbed. Using tongs, transfer to a plate and serve immediately.

Beef Stew

Servings: 8
Cooking Time: 1 Hour

Ingredients:

- 1 Tablespoon (15 ml) olive oil
- 2 pounds (907 g) Beef Stew meat , cut into 1-inch pieces
- 1 medium (1 medium) onion , chopped
- 4 cloves (4 cloves) garlic , minced
- 4 (4) carrots , cut into bite sized pieces
- 1 pound (454 g) potatoes , cut into bite sized pieces
- 2 stalks (2 stalks) celery , chopped
- 2 cups (480 ml) beef broth
- 14 ounces (397 g) tomato sauce (about 1 3/4 cups)
- 2 Tablespoons (30 ml) Worcestershire sauce (or soy sauce)
- 1 teaspoon (5 ml) dried herbs (thyme, oregano, basil)
- 1 Tablespoon (15 ml) sugar
- 1 teaspoon (5 ml) salt , or to taste

- 1/2 teaspoon (2.5 ml) black pepper
- 3 Tablespoons (45 ml) corn starch
- 3 Tablespoons (45 ml) water

Directions:
1. Turn Instant Pot on "Sauté" setting and add the olive oil. Stir in the onions & garlic and cook for 3-5 minutes or until softened and slightly browned.
2. Add the beef, carrots, potatoes, celery, beef broth, tomato sauce, Worcestershire sauce (or soy sauce), dried herbs, sugar, salt and black pepper. Stir to combine everything evenly.
3. Close the lid, making sure the vent is closed on the lid, and pressure cook on high pressure for 45 minutes. (These are the steps we did for our Instant Pot - Press "Cancel" to stop the "Sauté" setting. Press the "Manual" button. Set the time to 45 minutes.)
4. After the cooking time is complete, press "Cancel" and carefully release the pressure. Once pressure completely releases, whisk together the corn starch and water until all lumps are dissolved.
5. Open lid and add the corn starch/water mixture.
6. Gently stir the cornstarch slurry into the beef stew and close the lid for about 5 minutes for the gravy to thicken. Once gravy thickens, enjoy!

Air Fryer London Broil

Servings: 4
Cooking Time: 8 Minutes

Ingredients:
- 1 1/2 pounds top round London Broil
- 1 teaspoon olive oil
- 2 teaspoons Montreal Steak Seasoning

Directions:
1. Preheat your air fryer to 400 degrees.
2. Rub the beef down with oil then sprinkle it with Montreal Steak seasoning.
3. Place the London broil in the air fryer and cooked for 8 to 10 minutes, depending on the thickness of the steak, until the meat reaches desired doneness (this timing is for medium-rare).
4. Remove the London broil from the air fryer, allow it to rest for 10 minutes before slicing and serving, then enjoy!

NOTES
HOW TO COOK FROZEN LONDON BROIL IN THE AIR FRYER:
Preheat your air fryer to 400 degrees.
Rub the beef with oil and sprinkle Montreal Steak seasoning on both sides.
Place the frozen London broil in the air fryer and cook for 12 to 15 minutes.
HOW TO REHEAT LONDON BROIL IN THE AIR FRYER:
Preheat your air fryer to 350 degrees.
Cook the leftover London broil for 1 minute (for slices) or 2 to 3 minutes (for a slab) until warmed thoroughly.

Air Fryer New York Strip Steak

Servings: 2
Cooking Time: 12 Minutes

Ingredients:
- 2 New York strip steaks, 1½ inches thick, room temperature
- 1 tablespoon extra-virgin olive oil
- 1 teaspoon House Seasoning

Directions:
1. Rub steak with oil on both sides, and sprinkle steak on both sides with House Seasoning. Place steaks in air fryer basket, set temperature to 400 degrees, and cook for 6 minutes on each side for medium rare.
2. Serve warm with your favorite topping or steak sauce.

Air Fryer Grilled Ham And Cheese

Servings: 2
Cooking Time: 5 Minutes

Ingredients:
- 4 slices bread any kind
- 2 thick slices ham or 4 slices deli ham
- 4 ounces cheddar cheese sliced
- 2 teaspoons mustard
- 2 tablespoons butter

Directions:
1. Preheat air fryer to 350°F.
2. Place the mustard, ham, and cheddar between two slices of bread.
3. Butter the outside of each sandwich.
4. Place in the air fryer and use a toothpick to hold the sandwich in place.
5. Cook 4-6 minutes or until golden on the outside and melted inside.

Notes

Prep ahead and store in the refrigerator for 2-3 days until ready to cook.

Reheat leftovers in a 325°F air fryer for 4 minutes or until heated through. Use a toothpick to hold the sandwich in place.

SALADS & SIDE DISHES RECIPES

Air Fryer Roasted Garlic & Rosemary Potatoes

Servings: 4
Cooking Time: 15 Minutes

Ingredients:
- 1 pound mini gold & red yukon potatoes
- 2 tablespoons olive oil
- 3 garlic cloves minced
- ½ teaspoon dried thyme
- ½ teaspoon dried rosemary
- ½ teaspoon kosher salt
- ¼ teaspoon pepper

Directions:
1. Preheat Air Fryer to 350°F.
2. Rinse and halve potatoes.
3. In a large bowl, combine olive oil, garlic, thyme, rosemary, salt, and pepper.
4. Add potatoes and toss in the herb mixture.
5. Put potatoes in a single layer in the air fryer basket.
6. Cook for 13-15 minutes shaking the basket halfway through the cooking time.

Air-fryer Brussels Sprouts Salad With Spiced Maple Vinaigrette

Servings: 4

Ingredients:
- 1 lb. brussels sprouts, trimmed, halved lengthwise
- 6 Tbsp. extra-virgin olive oil, divided
- ½ tsp. Diamond Crystal or ¼ tsp. Morton kosher salt, plus more
- ½ cup coarsely chopped raw walnuts
- 1 tsp. crushed fennel seeds
- 1 tsp. nigella seeds
- 5 Tbsp. white wine vinegar or apple cider vinegar
- 2 Tbsp. pure maple syrup
- Freshly ground pepper
- ½ small red onion, halved, thinly sliced
- 5 oz. mixed salad greens or baby kale
- 1½ cups cooked grains (such as farro or barley)
- ¾ cup crumbled feta
- ¼ cup sweetened dried cranberries or dried tart cherries

Directions:
1. Heat air fryer to 400°. Toss 1 lb. brussels sprouts, trimmed, halved lengthwise, 3 Tbsp. extra-virgin olive oil, and ½ tsp. Diamond Crystal or ¼ tsp. Morton kosher salt in a large bowl to coat. Transfer to air fryer; reserve bowl. Roast, giving basket a shake halfway through, until tender, 18–20 minutes. Add ½ cup coarsely chopped raw walnuts and toss to combine. Roast until brussels sprouts are deep golden brown and charred in spots and walnuts are golden brown, about 2 minutes.
2. Meanwhile, toast 1 tsp. crushed fennel seeds and 1 tsp. nigella seeds in a dry small skillet over medium-high heat until fragrant, 30–45 seconds. Immediately transfer to a small bowl and add remaining 3 Tbsp. extra-virgin olive oil. Whisk in 5 Tbsp. white wine vinegar or apple cider vinegar and 2 Tbsp. pure maple syrup; season dressing with salt and freshly ground pepper.
3. Transfer brussels sprouts to reserved bowl. Add ½ small red onion, halved, thinly sliced, 5 oz. mixed salad greens or baby kale, 1½ cups cooked grains (such as farro or barley), ¾ cup crumbled feta, and ¼ cup sweetened dried cranberries or dried tart cherries. Drizzle dressing over salad and toss to coat.

Air Fryer Garlic & Herb Potato Wedges

Servings: 4
Cooking Time: 15 Minutes

Ingredients:
- 4 potatoes, sliced into wedges
- 1 tsp Italian seasoning
- 1/4 tsp salt
- 1/4 tsp pepper
- 1/2 tsp garlic powder
- 1/2 tsp onion powder
- 1 tbs olive oil

Directions:
1. Preheat the air fryer to 200°C.
2. Place the wedges in a medium sized bowl. Sprinkle with herbs, salt, pepper, garlic, and onion powder, and olive oil. Spread the wedges evenly inside the air fryer basket. Do not overcrowd.
3. Bake in the air fryer for 15 minutes, tossing halfway through the cooking process.

Crispy Garlic, Scallion, & Sesame Potato Wedges

Servings: 4

Ingredients:
- Potatoes
- 3 russet potatoes, cut into 1-inch-thick wedges
- 1 tablespoon neutral-flavored oil
- 1 teaspoon sesame oil
- 2 teaspoons kosher salt, plus more as needed
- Garlic-Scallion Oil
- 4 garlic cloves, finely minced
- 2 scallions, thinly sliced
- 1 tablespoon fresh ginger, grated
- 3 tablespoons sesame oil
- 1 tablespoon neutral oil
- 1 tablespoon rice wine vinegar
- ½ teaspoon red pepper flakes

Directions:
1. Toss the cut potato wedges with the neutral oil, sesame oil, and salt in a medium bowl until evenly coated.
2. Place the crisper plate into the Smart Air Fryer basket, then place the potato wedges onto the crisper plate.
3. Select the Fries function and press Start/Pause.
4. Combine all of the garlic-scallion oil ingredients in a small saucepan over medium heat and cook for 3—4 minutes or until simmering, then remove from heat.
5. Pour the garlic scallion oil over the potato wedges.
6. Select the Broil function, adjust time to 3 minutes, then press Start/Pause.
7. Remove when done, season with kosher salt to taste, and serve warm.

Colcannon

Servings: 6
Cooking Time: 18 Minutes

Ingredients:
- 2 slices bacon, cut into ¼-inch pieces
- ½ tablespoon olive oil
- ½ leek, white part only, finely chopped
- 4 green onions, green and white parts, finely chopped
- 5 garlic cloves, chopped
- ¼ Savoy cabbage, very thinly sliced
- ½ bunch curly kale, ribs removed and finely chopped
- 6 to 8 large Yukon gold potatoes, peeled and large diced
- 1½ cups chicken stock
- ¾ cup heavy cream
- 3 tablespoons unsalted butter
- ⅛ teaspoon ground nutmeg
- Kosher salt, to taste

Directions:
1. Select the Sauté function on the Pressure Cooker and adjust the time to 12 minutes and the temperature setting to 336°F, then press Start.

2. Place the bacon into the inner pot and sauté for 6 minutes, then remove to a plate. Drain all but one teaspoon of the rendered bacon fat out of the inner pot.
3. Add the olive oil into the inner pot, followed by the leek, green onions, and garlic. Sauté for 3 minutes, until fragrant and softened, then stir in the cabbage and curly kale and sauté for an additional 3 minutes, until softened.
4. Stir in the potatoes, then pour in the chicken stock.
5. Place the lid onto the pressure cooker and slide the steam release switch to Seal.
6. Select the Pressure Cook function, adjust pressure to high and time to 6 minutes, then press Start.
7. Release pressure quickly by sliding the steam release switch to Vent.
8. Open the lid carefully and mash the potatoes with a spoon, then stir in the heavy cream, butter, nutmeg, and bacon. Season the colcannon to taste with kosher salt, then serve.

Warm Roasted Potato & Bacon Salad

Servings: 4

Ingredients:
- 750g baby new potatoes, cut in half if large
- 1 tbsp olive oil
- 1 tbsp flaked sea salt
- fresh cracked pepper, as desired
- 3 slices of smoked bacon, cut into 1cm pieces
- 2 celery stalks, cut into 1cm slices
- 3 spring onions, sliced thin
- 40g mayonnaise
- 50g sour cream
- 2 tsp white vinegar
- COOKING MODE
- When entering cooking mode - We will enable your screen to stay 'always on' to avoid any unnecessary interruptions whilst you cook!

Directions:

1. Insert crisper plate in pan and place pan in unit. Preheat unit by selecting AIR FRY, set temperature to 180°C and set time to 3 minutes. Select START/STOP to begin.
2. Toss potatoes with oil, salt and pepper as desired.
3. Once unit has preheated, add potatoes to pan. Select AIR FRY, set temperature to 180°C and set time for 25 minutes. Select START/STOP to begin.
4. After 10 minutes, remove pan, add bacon to potatoes and shake pan liberally to mix ingredients. Reinsert pan to resume cooking.
5. After 20 minutes, remove pan and check potatoes are cooked. If desired, cook for up to an additional 5 minutes to crisp the potatoes.
6. When cooking is complete, remove pan and add potatoes to large bowl with remaining ingredients. Mix well and serve warm.

Grilled Beets With Whipped Ricotta & Herbs

Servings: 4

Ingredients:
- 2 large beets, peeled and sliced into ¼-inch rounds
- 2½ tablespoons olive oil, divided, plus more for drizzling
- 3 teaspoons kosher salt, divided
- 1½ cups whole milk ricotta cheese
- ¼ cup fresh mint leaves, chopped, for topping
- ¼ cup fresh basil leaves, chopped, for topping
- Freshly ground black pepper, for seasoning
- Flaky sea salt, for seasoning
- Items Needed:
- Food processor fitted with the blade attachment or blender

Directions:
1. Place the cooking pot into the base of the Indoor Grill, followed by the grill grate.
2. Select the Air Grill function on max heat, press Shake, then press Start/Pause to preheat.
3. Toss the beets with 1 tablespoon of olive oil and 1 teaspoon of salt in a large bowl.

4. Place the beets onto the preheated grill grate, then close the lid.
5. Flip the beets halfway through cooking. The Shake Reminder will let you know when.
6. Combine the ricotta cheese and remaining olive oil and salt in a food processor fitted with the blade attachment or a blender. Blend until very smooth, then scoop into a serving bowl and chill until ready to serve.
7. Remove the beets from the grill when done and let cool slightly.
8. Serve the beets on top of the whipped ricotta, topped with the fresh mint and basil and drizzled with olive oil. Season with pepper and flaky sea salt.

Salmon & Quinoa Salad

Servings: 4

Cooking Time: 9 Minutes

Ingredients:
- Salmon Salad:
- 4 frozen salmon filets
- 1 tablespoon olive oil
- 1 teaspoon kosher salt
- 1 cup cooked quinoa, room temperature
- 1 avocado, diced
- 1 cucumber, quartered & diced
- ¼ red onion, thinly sliced
- 6 cups mixed greens
- 1/4 cup feta cheese, crumbled
- Lemon Vinaigrette:
- 1 lemon, zested and juiced
- 1 tablespoon red wine vinegar
- 1 tablespoon minced fresh chives
- ¼ cup olive oil
- Kosher salt & black pepper, to taste

Directions:
1. Select Preheat on the Air Fryer, adjust the temperature to 360°F, then press Start/Pause.
2. Place the salmon filets into the air fryer skin side down.
3. Set the temperature to 360°F and time to 3 minutes, then press Start/Pause.
4. Open the basket, brush the salmon with olive oil and season it with salt and pepper.
5. Set the temperature to 360°F and time to 7 minutes, then press Start/Pause.
6. Place the remaining salad ingredients into a large bowl and toss together, then set aside.
7. Combine the lemon juice, red wine vinegar, and chives in a small bowl and whisk together. Slowly pour in the ¼ cup olive oil while whisking constantly until the dressing is emulsified, then season to taste with salt and pepper. Pour the dressing over the salad and toss to coat.
8. Remove the salmon from the air fryer when done. Divide the salad and salmon filets among four plates, then serve.

Air Fryer Chicken Milanese With Mediterranean Salad

Servings: 4

Cooking Time: 15 Minutes

Ingredients:
- Chicken
- 8 boneless thin sliced chicken breast fillets (about 4 ounces each, 1/4 inch thick)
- 1 teaspoon salt
- 1 1/2 cup panko (or gluten-free panko)
- 1/3 cup finely grated parmesan cheese
- 2 large eggs (beaten)
- olive oil spray
- Salad
- 5 cups 1 large head romaine lettuce, chopped
- 1 heirloom tomato (diced)
- 1/2 small red onion (chopped)
- 2 ounces grated feta cheese (grated from 1 block)
- Dressing
- 2 tablespoons fresh lemon juice
- 2 tablespoons red wine vinegar
- 1 tablespoon dried oregano
- 1 garlic clove (grated)

- 1/2 teaspoon kosher salt
- 2 tablespoons extra virgin olive oil

Directions:
1. Season the cutlets on both sides with salt.
2. In a shallow bowl combine the bread crumbs and parmesan cheese.
3. Beat the egg with 1 tablespoon water. Place in a large flat dish. Coat the cutlets with the egg mixture, remove the excess and dip them into crumbs.
4. Place the cutlets on a work surface and spray both sides generously with oil.
5. Air fry in batches 400F 6 to 7 minutes turning halfway, until the crumbs are golden brown and the center is no longer pink. Divide on 4 plates.
6. Make the dressing: Combine the lemon juice, vinegar, oregano, garlic, and 1/2 teaspoon salt and let sit until the oregano has absorbed some liquid, about 5 minutes. Whisk in the olive oil.
7. While the cutlets are cooking, toss all the lettuce, tomato, red onion and 1/4 teaspoon salt together in a large bowl. Drizzle over the dressing, toss, and divide among the 4 plates of chicken, piling it over the cutlets.
8. Using a box grater, grate 1/2 ounce of the cheese over each salad.

Notes
Variations:
If you don't have panko, you can use breadcrumbs.
Swap romaine lettuce for mixed greens.
Add avocado or cucumber for extra vegetables.

Air Fryer Peppers And Onions

Ingredients:
- 3 bell peppers seeded and cut lengthwise into ½-inch slices
- 1 red onion peeled and cut lengthwise into ½-inch slices
- 1 white onion peeled and cut lengthwise
- 1½ tbsp extra virgin olive oil
- 1½ tsp sea salt
- ⅛ tsp ground black pepper
- 1 tsp garlic powder
- ¼ tsp red pepper flakes

Directions:
1. Carefully slice the peppers and onions.
2. Add the pepper and onion slices to a large bowl.
3. Top the onions and peppers with olive oil, salt, pepper, garlic powder, and red pepper flakes.
4. Prepare the basket of the air fryer with nonstick cooking spray if needed.
5. Add the peppers and onions to the basket of the air fryer and air fry on 400 F/200 C for 15 minutes or until they've reached the desired tenderness.
6. Stir the peppers and onion halfway through the cooking process.
7. Serve immediately.

Air Fryer Smashed Potatoes

Servings: 4
Cooking Time: 12 Minutes

Ingredients:
- 24 ounces bag of baby red potatoes
- 2 tablespoons olive oil
- 1 tablespoon minced garlic
- salt and pepper to taste

Directions:
1. Wash and scrub your potatoes. Place them in a pot filled with cold water. Bring the water to a boil. Boil the potatoes till they are tender enough to be poked with a fork, about 15-20 minutes.
2. Combine your olive oil and garlic. Then preheat your air fryer to 400 degrees.
3. Drain your potatoes and then using a fork, smash them slightly. Brush them with the olive oil and garlic and sprinkle salt and pepper on top of them. Gently place them in your air fryer allowing a little room around each of them to allow full crispiness.
4. Cook for 10-13 minutes until they are nice and crispy. Top with parsley if desired and serve. Adjust time for larger potatoes or different air fryers.

NOTES
HOW TO REHEAT SMASHED POTATOES:
Place your potatoes in your air fryer at 370 degrees for 4 minutes or until heated thoroughly.

VEGETABLE & & VEGETARIAN RECIPES

Spinach Artichoke Zucchini Bites

Servings: 2

Ingredients:
- 4 oz. cream cheese, softened
- 2/3 c. shredded mozzarella
- 1/4 c. freshly grated Parmesan
- 1/2 c. canned artichoke hearts, drained and chopped
- 1/2 c. frozen spinach, thawed and drained
- 2 tbsp. sour cream
- 2 cloves garlic, minced
- Pinch crushed red pepper flakes
- Kosher salt
- Freshly ground black pepper
- 3 medium zucchini, cut into 1/2" rounds

Directions:
1. FOR OVEN
2. Preheat oven to 400° and line a large baking sheet with parchment paper. In a medium bowl, combine cream cheese, mozzarella, Parmesan, artichokes, spinach, sour cream, garlic, and crushed red pepper. Season with salt and pepper.
3. Spread about a tablespoon of cream cheese mixture on top of each zucchini coin.
4. Bake until zucchini is tender and cheese is melty, 15 minutes. For more color, broil on high, 1 to 2 minutes.
5. FOR AIR FRYER
6. In a medium bowl, combine cream cheese, mozzarella, Parmesan, artichokes, spinach, sour cream, garlic, and crushed red pepper. Season with salt and pepper. Set aside.
7. Cook zucchini slices in air fryer at 375° for 8 minutes then top each slice with 1 tablespoon cream cheese mixture.
8. Return to air fryer and continue cooking in batches until cheese is deeply golden and zucchini is tender, about 10 minutes more.

Air Fryer Cauliflower Wings

Servings: 4

Cooking Time: 18 Minutes

Ingredients:
- 1 cup rice flour
- ½ cup all-purpose flour
- 1 tablespoon cornstarch
- 1 teaspoon baking powder
- 1 teaspoon kosher salt
- 1 ¼ cups cold club soda
- 1 head cauliflower cut into florets
- ⅓ cup BBQ sauce
- 3 tablespoons non-dairy butter
- ½ teaspoon red pepper flakes optional, to taste

Directions:
1. Preheat the air fryer basket to 400°F for 5 minutes.
2. In a large bowl, whisk together the rice flour, all-purpose flour, cornstarch, baking powder, and kosher salt. Add the club soda and whisk until no large lumps remain.
3. Spray the preheated air fryer basket with olive oil spray and then carefully dip a cauliflower floret into the batter and place it in the air fryer. Repeat with as many florets as will fit, but make sure not to overcrowd the air fryer. Be careful– the air fryer is hot!
4. Cook at 400°F for 12 minutes. Flip the cauliflower and cook for an additional 8 minutes. Between batches, keep the cauliflower on a cooling rack set over a baking sheet– this will help keep it crispy until you're ready to sauce it.
5. Meanwhile, add the BBQ sauce, non-dairy butter, and red pepper flakes to a large microwave-safe bowl. Cook for 1 minute, or until the butter is melted, and then whisk to combine.
6. Toss the cooked cauliflower in the sauce and then return it to the air fryer. Cook for an additional 5 minutes.

7. Serve immediately garnished with chopped green onion or parsley.

Notes

These cauliflower wings are best enjoyed immediately after they are cooked as they will become soggy as they sit.

Rice flour is the key to crispy cauliflower wings— it helps create a mock tempura batter that stays crispier than a typical flour batter. If you don't have rice flour, a gluten-free flour substitute will work as well.

These wings will keep in an airtight container in the refrigerator for 3-5 days.

Air Fryer Broccoli

Servings: 4
Cooking Time: 6 Minutes

Ingredients:

- 1 head Broccoli cut into about 3-4 cups
- 2 tablespoons olive oil
- 1/2 teaspoon garlic powder
- 1/4 teaspoon salt
- 1/4 teaspoon black pepper
- Optional Toppings: Shredded Cheese, such as parmesan or cheddar

Directions:

1. Cut broccoli before air frying, slice the broccoli head and cut broccoli florets, medium to small in sized pieces, removing the core.
2. Place florets in a medium Bowl. Add the olive oil, garlic powder, salt, and pepper. Toss the broccoli until it is coated with the oil and Seasonings.
3. Transfer the seasoned broccoli to basket, in a single layer, work in batches if necessary.
4. Air fry broccoli at 400° Fahrenheit for 5-7 minutes, shake air fryer basket halfway through cooking, and cook until broccoli reaches your the crisp you desire.

NOTES

If topping with cheese, add immediately to cooked broccoli is done so that it lightly melts, or you can add cheese to broccoli one minute before cooking time is done so that it is melted.

Air Fryer Spicy Cauliflower

Servings: 4
Cooking Time: 18 Minutes

Ingredients:

- 1 small head cauliflower (about 1 1/2 lbs. - 680g), cut into bite sized pieces
- 2 Tablespoons (30 ml) vegetable oil
- 2 Tablespoons (30 ml) hot sauce
- 1 Tablespoon (15 ml) soy sauce
- 1 Tablespoon (15 ml) rice vinegar
- 1 teaspoon (5 ml) sesame seed oil
- Lime wedges, optional for serving
- salt, optional to taste
- black pepper, optional to taste
- Fresh chopped herbs (such as mint, cilantro, Thai basil), optional for serving

Directions:

1. Put the cauliflower in a large bowl. Add the oil, hot sauce, soy sauce, rice vinegar and sesame seed oil to the cauliflower. Toss the cauliflower with the sauce until it completely soaks it all up (there shouldn't be any sauce left pooling at the bottom of the bowl).
2. Put the cauliflower in the air fryer basket/tray and spread evenly.
3. Air Fry at 360°F/182°C for 10 minutes. Gently shake or turn the cauliflower.
4. Continue to Air Fry for another 2-8 minutes or cooked to your preferred texture.
5. Taste for seasoning & add salt & pepper or other seasonings if desired. Serve with optional lime wedges and topped with optional chopped herbs. Enjoy!!

Air Fried Oyster Mushrooms

Servings: 8
Cooking Time: 15 Minutes

Ingredients:
- 7 oz (200 g) oyster mushrooms
- 3/4 cup (180 g) dairy-free milk
- 1/2 Tbsp apple cider vinegar
- 1/2 cup (50 g) chickpea flour
- Breading
- 1 cup (90 g) oats ground into a coarse flour (see notes)
- 3 Tbsp (15 g) nutritional yeast (see notes)
- 1 1/4 tsp salt
- 1 tsp smoked paprika
- 1 tsp onion powder
- 1 tsp garlic powder
- 1/2 tsp cumin
- Black pepper to taste
- Cooking spray

Directions:
1. You can watch the video in the post for visual instructions.
2. First, gently clean each oyster mushroom with a damp paper towel or cloth.
3. Then, combine the dairy-free milk, vinegar, and chickpea flour in a bowl. Set aside for some minutes. Meanwhile, mix all the breading ingredients in a large bowl.
4. Working one at a time, coat an oyster mushroom in the wet mixture, then the breading, and repeat once more, so it's thoroughly coated. Repeat with the remaining mushrooms.
5. Spray your air fryer basket* with cooking spray and add a single layer of the mushrooms with space in between (cook in batches if necessary). Spray them generously with cooking spray. This will help them become crispy.
6. *Check the FAQs in the post for the oven and skillet method.
7. Air fry the mushrooms for 14-16 minutes at 360 °F/180 °C, flipping them every 5 minutes and spraying them lightly with cooking spray each time.
8. Serve with this Yum Yum Sauce and enjoy!

Notes
Oats: You can use breadcrumbs (regular or GF) instead of oats.
Nutrition: al yeast Will add a cheesy/umami flavor. If you don't want to use it, add a little mushroom powder or just add more spices.

Air Fryer Corn On The Cob

Servings: 4

Ingredients:
- 4 ears of corn, shucked, halved if necessary
- 1 c. finely crumbled feta
- 3 tbsp. finely chopped red onion
- 2 tsp. finely chopped fresh basil, plus more for serving
- 1 1/4 tsp. dried oregano
- 1/2 c. full-fat plain Greek yogurt
- 1/2 tsp. sweet or smoked paprika
- Lemon wedges, for serving

Directions:
1. Working in batches if necessary, in an air-fryer basket, arrange corn in a single layer. Cook at 400°, turning halfway through, until bright yellow and tender, 10 to 12 minutes.
2. Meanwhile, in a medium bowl, mix feta, onion, basil, and oregano until well combined.
3. Spread 2 tablespoons yogurt onto each cob, then top with feta mixture. Sprinkle with paprika and garnish with more basil. Serve warm or at room temperature with lemon wedges alongside.

Air Fryer Tofu

Servings: 4
Cooking Time: 12 Minutes

Ingredients:
- 1 block extra-firm tofu (12 to 15 ounces) must be extra firm
- 3 tablespoons low sodium soy sauce
- 1 tablespoon rice wine vinegar
- 1 tablespoon pure maple syrup
- 2 teaspoons extra virgin olive oil
- 1 teaspoon garlic powder
- 1/2 teaspoon ground ginger
- 1/2 teaspoon Sriracha or hot sauce of choice
- 1 tablespoon corn starch or arrowroot starch

Directions:
1. Remove the tofu from the package and drain. With your hands, gently squeeze out as much water as possible without breaking or crushing the block. Lay the tofu flat on a cutting board, so the longer edge is towards you, then cut it into four strips. Rotate the strips so that the wider (cut sides) are flat against the cutting board, and cut them in half again, so you have 8 strips total. Cut the strips crosswise into 1-inch cubes (I end up with 5 cubes per strip).
2. Line a cutting board or large plate with a clean tea towel (or similar lint-free kitchen towel) or paper towels. Spread the tofu cubes onto it in one layer and lay a second towel on top. Press gently but firmly and change out the towel as needed. The idea is to remove as much water from the tofu as possible.
3. In a small bowl or large liquid measuring cup, stir together the soy sauce, vinegar, syrup, oil, garlic powder, ginger, and hot sauce.
4. Place the tofu in a shallow baking dish or medium mixing bowl. Pour the soy sauce mixture over the tofu, then with your hand, toss gently to combine. Let the tofu sit for 15 minutes, tossing it again halfway through. Don't worry if a few bits crumble. Those will turn deliciously crispy.
5. If you'd like to keep the tofu warm between batches, preheat your oven to 250 degrees F and line a baking sheet with parchment paper. Preheat the air fryer to 400 degrees F according to the manufacturer's instructions (for my air fryer, that is 3 minutes of preheat time).
6. Just before cooking, sprinkle the corn starch evenly over the top of the tofu and toss to coat.
7. Coat the basket of the air fryer with nonstick spray. Add the tofu in one layer, leaving a little space around the cubes so they do not touch and the air can circulate. (Depending upon the size of your air fryer, you may need to cook it in two or three batches.)
8. Cook the tofu for 9 minutes. Then slide the basket out, and shake it gently to toss the tofu. Continue to cook for 2 to 4 additional minutes, tossing and checking it each minute, until the tofu is crisp and dark golden. (The time will vary based on your air fryer; keep a close eye on it towards the end to ensure it doesn't burn.) If desired, transfer the tofu to the baking sheet and keep it warm in the oven while you finish the rest.
9. Repeat with remaining tofu, discarding any excess marinade (if you have some crumbled bits of tofu in the bottom of the bowl, you can air fry those too). Enjoy!

Notes

TO MAKE GLUTEN FREE: Use tamari, coconut aminos, or liquid aminos in place of the soy sauce.

TO STORE: Refrigerate tofu in an airtight storage container for up to 4 days.

TO REHEAT: Recrisp tofu in the air fryer at 375 degrees F. It will only take a few minutes, so check often to prevent burning.

TO FREEZE: The texture of the tofu may change once frozen and thawed, but the flavor will remain delicious. Place tofu cubes in a single layer on a parchment-lined baking sheet. Freeze until solid. Freeze the frozen tofu in an airtight, freezer-safe storage container for up to 3 months. Let thaw overnight in the refrigerator before reheating.

Air Fryer Fried Pickles

Servings: 3

Ingredients:
- 2 c. dill pickle slices
- 1/2 c. plain bread crumbs
- 1/4 c. finely grated Parmesan
- 1 tsp. dried oregano
- 1 tsp. garlic powder
- 1 large egg, whisked with 1 tbsp. water
- Ranch dressing, for serving

Directions:
1. Pat pickle slices dry with paper towels. In a medium bowl, stir bread crumbs, Parmesan, oregano, and garlic powder.
2. Dredge pickles in egg, then in bread crumb mixture. Transfer to a plate.
3. Working in batches, in an air-fryer basket, arrange pickles in a single layer. Cook at 400° until golden brown and crisp, about 10 minutes.
4. Serve with ranch dressing alongside.

Air-fryer Roast Potatoes Recipe

Servings: 4

Cooking Time: 30 Minutes

Ingredients:
- 1kg King Edward potatoes, peeled and cut into 3cm
- 2 sprigs of fresh rosemary (optional)
- 2-3 whole garlic cloves, unpeeled
- 2 tbsp rapeseed oil
- large pinch of flaky sea salt

Directions:
1. Bring a large pan of water to the boil. Add the potatoes, return to the boil and cook for 8 mins. Drain well and return to the dry pan.
2. Preheat the air-fryer to 200°C.
3. Shake the pan to roughen the edges of the potatoes, then add the rosemary and garlic. Drizzle over the oil and sprinkle with salt, then shake to coat.
4. Tip into the air-fryer basket and cook for 18-20 mins, shaking after 10 mins, until golden brown at the edges. Serve hot.

Air Fryer Radishes

Servings: 4

Cooking Time: 10 Minutes

Ingredients:
- 1 bunch radishes, washed, trimmed and quartered (about 12-15 radishes)
- 2 tablespoons olive oil
- ½ teaspoon garlic powder
- ½ teaspoon salt
- ¼ teaspoon black pepper
- Fresh parsley for garnish (optional)

Directions:
1. Preheat air fryer to 400 F.
2. In a medium bowl, toss the chopped radishes with olive oil and seasonings until everything is uniformly mixed.
3. Add the radishes to the air fryer in a single layer and cook 8-10 minutes, shaking the basket at the halfway mark, or until tender on the inside.

Air Fryer Baked Potato

Servings: 4

Cooking Time: 25 Minutes

Ingredients:

4 large russet potatoes * See **notes**
- 2 tablespoons butter melted
- 1/2 teaspoon salt
- 1/4 teaspoon pepper

Directions:
1. Scrub the potatoes, then pat them dry.
2. Poke the potatoes all over with a fork, then rub the melted butter over each potato and season with salt and pepper.
3. Cook the potatoes at 200C/400F for 30-35 minutes, flip, and cook for an additional 5-10 minutes.
4. Transfer the potatoes onto a plate. Cut the potatoes in the middle and fill generously with sour cream,

followed by shredded cheese, chopped bacon, and green onions.

Notes

* Please refer to the cooking time and potato size conversion below-

8 oz or less: 30-35 minutes.

9 oz to 12 oz: 35-40 minutes.

12 oz to 14 oz: 45-50 minutes.

14 oz to 16 oz: 55-60 minutes.

Over 16 oz: At least 60 minutes, and en extra 5 minutes for each ounce over 16.

TO STORE: Place leftovers in airtight containers and store in the refrigerator for 3-4 days.

TO FREEZE: Place the cooked and cooled potatoes in freezer-safe bags and store in the freezer for up to 3 months.

TO REHEAT: Reheat in the microwave, oven or air fryer.

Air Fryer Twice Baked Potatoes

Servings: 4
Cooking Time: 15 Minutes

Ingredients:

- 2 large baking potatoes
- 1 tablespoon extra-virgin olive oil
- 3 tablespoons butter softened
- ¼ cup sour cream
- ¼ teaspoon garlic powder
- 2 slices bacon cooked and crumbled
- ¾ cup sharp cheddar cheese divided
- 2 green onions thinly sliced

Directions:

1. Scrub potatoes and pat dry. Poke with a fork, then rub with oil and season with salt.
2. Place potatoes in the air fryer and bake at 390°F for 45-50 minutes.
3. Remove from the air fryer and cool 15 minutes.
4. Cut potatoes in half lengthwise and scoop out the inside leaving a ½" shell.
5. Mash the potatoes in a bowl with sour cream, butter, and garlic powder. You can add a small amount of milk or cream if needed. Stir in ½ cup of the cheese, the bacon and green onions. Taste and season with salt and pepper.
6. Fill the potato shells with the filling and top with remaining cheese.
7. Cook at 390°F for 6-8 minutes or until the cheese is melted.

Notes

Add a small amount of milk or cream to the mashed potatoes if needed.

Avoid scraping too much from the shell, it needs to stay rigid enough to hold all the good stuff. A half-inch width is perfect.

Keep leftover twice-baked potatoes covered in the refrigerator for up to 5 days. Reheat them in the air fryer or microwave.

Make and chill portions in advance, wrap in plastic and freeze in zippered bags for future meals. Reheat from frozen in the air fryer and serve.

Air Fryer Roast Potatoes

Servings: 2
Cooking Time: 30 Minutes-1hour

Ingredients:

- 2 large floury potatoes (approximately 450g/1lb) (see Recipe Tip)
- salt, to taste
- 1 tbsp olive oil

Directions:

1. Peel and quarter the potatoes before par-boiling them in a saucepan of already boiling, salted water for 15 minutes.
2. Drain the potatoes well and leave them to steam dry for a minute or two before tossing with the olive oil and a generous seasoning of salt.
3. Air-fry for 30 minutes at 200C, tossing every 10 minutes to ensure they crisp up and brown evenly.

NOTES

This recipe was tested in a 3.2 litre/5½ pint basket air fryer. It will also work in a model fitted with a stirring paddle – in this case, you will not need to toss the potatoes during cooking. It is also easily scaled up to feed more people in a larger air fryer.

Large potatoes are best for this recipe, if you are using smaller potatoes make sure they are cut into large chunks or reduce the par-boil time.

Air Fryer Pesto Roast Potatoes

Servings: 2
Cooking Time: 28 Minutes

Ingredients:
- 2 large potatoes, approx. 370g
- 7 tsp dairy-free pesto
- 2 tsp lemon juice
- salt
- low-calorie cooking spray

Directions:
1. Preheat the air fryer to 190°C. Peel the potatoes and dice into pieces around 5cm in length. Place in a pan filled with cold water and add plenty of salt.
2. Bring the pan up to the boil and cook for 5-8 minutes, until they start to soften but are still firm.
3. Drain in a colander and leave them for 5 minutes. After 5 minutes give them a shake to fluff up the edges. Add back into the pan and add 6 tsp of pesto. Toss to coat.
4. Add the potatoes to the air fryer basket and spray with low-calorie cooking spray. Cook for 20 minutes, making sure to turn halfway.
5. In a small bowl combine the lemon juice with the remaining 1 tsp pesto. Once the roast potatoes are cooked, drizzle over the lemon juice and pesto and toss to coat.

Air Fryer Cheesy Potatoes

Servings: 4
Cooking Time: 25 Minutes

Ingredients:
- 4 Russet potatoes
- 2 tbsp olive oil
- 1 tsp paprika
- 1 tsp salt
- 1 tsp garlic powder
- ½ tsp black pepper
- ½ cup shredded Cheddar Jack cheese

Directions:
1. To make this recipe, begin by rinsing and then cutting the potatoes into wedges, leaving the potato skin on.
2. Add the cut potatoes to a medium bowl, and cover with cold water. Let them soak in the cold water for 25-30 minutes. This will remove the starch and makes them crispy.
3. Once they have soaked, drain the water and pat the sliced potatoes dry with paper towels. Return them to the bowl. 4. Coat potatoes with a tablespoon olive oil, paprika, salt, garlic powder, and pepper. Mix until coated evenly.
4. Place the seasoned potato wedges into a single layer in the air fryer basket, without overlapping.
5. Air fry the potatoes at 400 degrees Fahrenheit for 20-23 minutes
6. During the cooking process, shake the basket at the 10 minute mark. If you have larger wedges, you may need to add 2-3 extra minutes for cooking time.
7. Open the basket and sprinkle the cheese onto the potato wedges. Air fry the cheese covered potatoes at 400 degrees Fahrenheit for 2 minutes, or until the cheese is melted and starting to golden.
8. Remove the cheesy potatoes from the basket with a spatula and serve with ranch dipping sauce.

NOTES

Consider using fry sauce, ketchup, or other dipping sauced to serve with the cheesy potatoes.

Refrigerate leftovers in an airtight container in the refrigerator for up to 3 days.

Air Fryer Stuffed Mushrooms

Servings: 16
Cooking Time: 5 Minutes

Ingredients:
- 16 medium mushrooms
- 8 ounces cream cheese softened
- 2 tablespoons bacon crumbled, about 3 slices
- ⅓ cup cheddar cheese shredded, divided
- 2 tablespoons parmesan cheese grated
- ¼ teaspoon garlic powder
- ¼ teaspoon kosher salt or to taste
- ⅛ teaspoon smoked paprika
- 1 green onion thinly sliced

Directions:
1. Quickly rinse and dry mushrooms.
2. Remove the stem from the mushroom caps (and scoop out the center using a small spoon if desired).
3. Beat softened cream cheese with a mixer on medium until smooth and fluffy.
4. Add bacon, 3 tablespoons cheddar cheese, parmesan cheese, seasonings, and green onion.
5. Stuff the mixture into the mushroom caps.
6. Preheat air fryer to 400°F. Add mushrooms, reduce heat to 350°F. Cook mushrooms 6 minutes.
7. Open the air fryer and top mushrooms with remaining cheddar. Cook 2 minutes longer.
8. Cool 5 minutes before serving.

Notes

Depending on your air fryer, the mushrooms can fall sideways as you open/close it. If this is the case, place the mushrooms on a piece of foil and fold up the sides to hold them upright or place them in a small baking pan and place in the air fryer.

Air Fryer Veggie Tots

Servings: 4
Cooking Time: 10 Minutes

Ingredients:
- 20 veggie tots

Directions:
1. Preheat the air fryer to 400 degrees Fahrenheit. Prepare the basket of the air fryer with non-stick cooking spray such as olive oil or avocado oil.
2. Add the frozen tots in a single layer in the bottom of a prepared and preheated air fryer basket.
3. Air fry veggie tots at 400 degrees Fahrenheit for 8-10 minutes or until golden brown, tossing the tots halfway through the cooking time.
4. Carefully remove the veggie tots from the air fryer.
5. Serve with your favorite dipping sauce on a serving plate.

NOTES

This recipe was made with a basket-style Cosori 5.8qt Air Fryer. If you are using a different brand of air fryer, you may need to adjust the cooking time slightly. You can also use parchment paper to help keep the air fryer basket clean. If using parchment paper, make sure to preheat the air fryer BEFORE placing the parchment paper into the air fryer.

OPTIONAL TOTS: You can grab different vegetable tots such as frozen cauliflower veggie tots, broccoli cheese tots, sweet potato tots, zucchini tots, and air fryer broccoli tots.

OPTIONAL TOPPINGS: You can change up the flavors by sprinkling the cooked veggie tots with parmesan cheese or different seasonings such as onion powder or garlic powder.

Air Fryer Vegetables

Servings: 4

Ingredients:

- 400g potatoes, cut into small chunks roughly 1 inch across
- 2 carrots, peeled and cut into 1.5 inch chunks
- 1 parsnip, peeled and cut into chunks (or add more carrots)
- 1 swede, peeled and cut into chunks (or add more carrots)
- 2 tbsp olive oil, divided
- 2 tsp smoked paprika (optional)
- 1 tsp garlic powder (optional)
- 1 tsp salt
- 1/2 tsp black pepper
- 1/2 tsp dried oregano
- 1 red onion (optional)

Directions:

1. Toss the Potatoes, Carrots, Parsnips and Swede in 2 tbsp Olive Oil and select air crisp. Set the timer for 15 minutes at 200 C.
2. Combine Smoked Paprika, Garlic, Salt, Pepper and Oregano in a large bowl.
3. Add the Potatoes, Carrots, Parsnips and Swede as well as the Onions to the bowl and toss in an additional 1 Tbsp Olive Oil.
4. Air crisp for an additional 5 – 7 minutes.

Air Fryer Buffalo Cauliflower

Servings: 4

Cooking Time: 13 Minutes

Ingredients:

- 1 large cauliflower chopped into equal sized florets
- 1 cup all purpose flour use gluten free, if needed
- 1 cup milk I used soy milk
- 1/2 teaspoon salt
- 1/2 teaspoon pepper
- 1 cup hot sauce I used Frank's Buffalo hot sauce

1/4 cup butter melted * See **notes**

Directions:

1. In a mixing bowl, add your flour, milk, salt, and pepper, and whisk until a smooth batter remains.
2. Moving quickly, dip the cauliflower into the batter until completely covered. Place the battered cauliflower in a single layer in the air fryer basket. Cook for 13-15 minutes at 200C/400F, or until crispy and golden brown.
3. While the cauliflower is cooking, prepare the sauce. In a mixing bowl, whisk together the buffalo hot sauce and melted butter until smooth.
4. Remove the crispy cauliflower from the air fryer and drench them in the buffalo sauce. Place them on a plate and serve immediately.

Notes

* vegan butter works.

TO STORE: Leftover cauliflower should be stored in the refrigerator, covered. It will keep well for up to 5 days.

TO FREEZE: Place the cauliflower in a shallow container and store it in the freezer for up to 2 months. Let it thaw completely before reheating.

TO REHEAT: Place a single layer of the thawed/chilled cauliflower in the air fryer and cook at 200C/400F for 5 minutes, flipping once halfway through.

Air Fryer Vegetable Peel Crisps

Servings: 4

Cooking Time: 35 Minutes

Ingredients:

- Peel of 3 potatoes (see tip)
- Peel of 1 orange sweet potato
- Peel of 1 orange sweet potato
- Greek yoghurt, to serve
- Chilli sauce, to serve
- lemon-herb salt
- 1 lemon
- 10cm fresh rosemary sprig
- 30g (1/4 cup) sea salt flakes
- Select all Ingredients:

Directions:

1. To make the lemon-herb salt, use a vegetable peeler to peel strips of rind lengthways (avoid the pith) from the lemon. Cut each strip in half lengthways. Place the peel and rosemary in the basket of an air fryer. Cook at 70C for 10 minutes. Remove the rosemary. Cook peel for a further 10-15 minutes or until dry. Remove and set aside to cool. Strip dried leaves from the rosemary sprig. Combine dried peel and rosemary leaves in a spice grinder or mortar, and grind to a powder. Add to a jar with the salt. Use the end of a wooden spoon to gently crush and combine.
2. Wash the vegetable peel and use a clean tea towel to thoroughly dry. Place in a bowl and spray lightly with olive oil. Toss to coat. Place in a single layer in the basket of the air fryer (you may need to do 2 batches). Cook at 180C, stopping to toss once or twice, for 8-10 minutes, or until dry. Transfer to a plate. Sprinkle with the herb salt to taste. Serve with yoghurt and chilli sauce.

NOTES
Use washed potatoes if possible, or scrub them very well to remove dirt if not.
Lemon-herb salt will keep in the pantry for up to 2 months. It's delicious on chicken or roast vegies.

Air Fryer Squash

Servings: 4
Cooking Time: 15 Minutes

Ingredients:
- 1 pound yellow squash
- 1 Tablespoon olive oil
- 1 teaspoon garlic powder
- 1/2 teaspoon ground black pepper
- 1 teaspoon fresh parsley optional garnish

Directions:
1. Prepare the squash by washing and chopping off the ends. Cut the squash into ¼-1/2" rounds.
2. Preheat the air fryer to 400 degrees Fahrenheit.
3. Add the cut squash into a small bowl and toss or brush with olive oil, garlic powder, and ground black pepper.
4. Add the squash to the basket of your air fryer. There may be a little overlapping. Try and allow as much air flow to each piece as possible.
5. Cook the squash for 13-15 minutes, tossing the rounds about halfway through the cooking time.
6. Garnish with fresh parsley or fresh herbs before serving.

NOTES
Try and keep the cut squash in a single layer in the air fryer basket so that the hot air can circulate throughout the basket and cook the squash evenly.
Keep the squash slices between ¼" and ½" in size. A mandolin is an easy way to cut them perfectly every time.
Add a little Italian seasoning for even more flavor.
This recipe was made using a Cosori air fryer. If you are using a different brand of air fryer, you may need to adjust the cooking time and temp slightly.

Air Fryer Brussels Sprouts

Servings: 8

Ingredients:
- 2 lb. Brussels sprouts, trimmed and halved
- 5 tbsp. olive oil, divided
- 1/2 tsp. hot paprika
- Kosher salt
- 6 tbsp. pure maple syrup
- 1 1/2 tbsp. sriracha
- Aleppo pepper and sliced scallions, for serving

Directions:
1. Heat air fryer to 375°F. In large bowl, toss Brussels sprouts with 4 tablespoons oil, then paprika and 1/2 teaspoon salt. Air-fry Brussels sprouts in 2 batches until charred, crispy, and tender, 9 to 11 minutes.
2. Meanwhile, in bowl, whisk together maple syrup, sriracha, and a pinch of salt. Transfer 2 1/2

tablespoons to small bowl and whisk in remaining tablespoon oil; set aside for serving.

3. Transfer 1 batch roasted Brussels sprouts to large bowl and toss with 2 tablespoons of remaining syrup mixture. Repeat with remaining Brussels sprouts and 2 tablespoons syrup mixture.
4. Transfer to platter, then drizzle with reserved maple-oil mixture and sprinkle with Aleppo pepper and scallions if desired.

Roasted Brussels Sprouts With Pancetta

Servings: 8

Ingredients:
- 2 pound Brussels sprouts
- 6 tablespoons olive oil
- 4 ounces pancetta, cut into ¼-in. cubes
- 2 teaspoons kosher salt
- ½ teaspoon freshly ground black pepper
- 1 teaspoon lemon zest (from 1 lemon)

Directions:
1. Preheat oven to 425°F with racks in upper and lower thirds. Trim Brussels sprouts and halve lengthwise, pulling off and reserving any loose outer leaves. Transfer Brussels sprouts and leaves to a large bowl.
2. Place 2 rimmed baking sheets in preheated oven on upper and lower racks; let heat until hot, about 5 minutes. Meanwhile, add oil, pancetta, salt, and pepper to Brussels sprouts in bowl; toss to coat.
3. Place hot baking sheets on a heatproof surface; divide Brussels sprouts mixture (including oil) evenly between them, carefully placing as many Brussels sprouts cut sides down as possible. Return baking sheets to oven; roast for 10 minutes. Rotate baking sheets from top to bottom; continue roasting until Brussels sprouts are deeply browned and leaves are browned and crispy, 6 to 8 minutes.
4. Remove Brussels sprouts from oven; sprinkle evenly with lemon zest and serve immediately. (To make ahead, let roasted Brussels sprouts stand, undisturbed, on baking sheets for up to 2 hours. Reheat at 350°F until crispy, 5 to 7 minutes, then garnish with lemon zest.)

NOTES

Cook, cut sides down, on already hot baking sheets for the best browning.

FAVORITE AIR FRYER RECIPES

'pups' In Blankets With Sprouts

Servings: 4

Ingredients:

- For the vegan bacon
- 1 aubergine, peeled & thinly sliced
- 4 tbsp olive oil
- 1 1/2 tsp smoked paprika
- 1/2 tsp each salt and pepper
- 1 1/2 tbsp maple syrup
- 1/4 tsp liquid smoke
- For the rest
- 1 pack vegan sausages
- 1 pack Brussel sprouts, washed, peeled & thinly sliced
- Toothpicks
- COOKING MODE
- When entering cooking mode - We will enable your screen to stay 'always on' to avoid any unnecessary interruptions whilst you cook!

Directions:

1. First prep the 'pups' in blankets. Mix all the ingredients for the Vegan Bacon, apart from the aubergine, into a wide bowl
2. Take a slice of aubergine & drip into the marinade, covering both sides
3. Slice your sausages in half
4. Wrap the aubergine around the sausage and use a toothpick to secure it
5. Add this to one of the draws in the Ninja Foodi Dual Zone Air Fryer. Cook at 190C for 15mins
6. Once the pups in blankets have been prepped, use the remaining aubergine and cut it into 'lardon' shape pieces
7. Add this to the bowl with the marinade and mix well
8. Add the Brussel sprouts in and mix all together
9. Add the mixture to the second drawer of the Ninja Foodi Dual Zone Air Fryer. Cook at 210C for 18 mins. You can use the Sync feature to get them both ready at the same time!

Air Fryer Frozen Mozzarella Sticks

Servings: 2

Cooking Time: 8 Minutes

Ingredients:

- 6 Frozen Mozzarella Sticks
- Dipping Sauce Options: Marinara sauce, ketchup, ranch, sweet chili sauce, mustard sauce, etc...
- EQUIPMENT
- Air Fryer

Directions:

1. Place the frozen mozzarella sticks in the air fryer basket and spread out evenly in a single layer. No oil spray is needed.
2. Air Fry at 380°F/193°C for 5 minutes. Gently shake or turn. Continue to Air Fry at 380°F/193°C for another 1-2 minutes OR until the cheese nearly starts to ooze out.
3. Make sure to let them cool a little before eating. The cheese can be super hot. Serve with your favorite dip.

NOTES

Nutrition: based on using Frozen Cauliflower Veggie Tots.

Air Frying Tips and Notes

No Oil Necessary. Cook Frozen - Do not thaw first.

Shake or turn if needed. Don't overcrowd the air fryer basket.

Recipe timing is based on a non-preheated air fryer. If cooking in multiple batches back to back, the following batches may cook a little quicker.

Recipes were tested in 3.7 to 6 qt. air fryers. If using a larger air fryer, they might cook quicker so adjust cooking time.

Remember to set a timer to shake/flip/toss as directed in recipe.

Air-fryer Mozzarella Sticks

Servings: 12
Cooking Time: 3 Minutes

Ingredients:

- ⅓ cup all-purpose flour
- 2 8 ounce pkg. mozzarella cheese, cut into 24 (2- to 2 1/2-inch) sticks
- 1 cup panko bread crumbs
- 1 tablespoon chopped fresh parsley
- ¼ teaspoon garlic powder
- 1 egg
- 1 tablespoon water
- Nonstick cooking spray
- Marinara sauce, warmed (optional)

Directions:

1. Place flour in a shallow dish. Dip cheese sticks into flour to coat. Arrange on a tray. Freeze for 1 hour.
2. In another shallow dish combine bread crumbs, parsley, and garlic powder. In a third shallow dish whisk together egg and the water. Dip cheese sticks again into flour and then into egg mixture, then into crumb mixture, turning to coat.
3. Coat air-fryer basket with cooking spray. Preheat air fryer at 400°F. Place cheese sticks, about six at a time, in prepared basket. Cook 3 minutes or until golden. Transfer to a plate. Serve warm. If desired, serve with marinara sauce.
4. To Make Ahead
5. Coat cheese sticks as directed in step 2 and place on a tray or plate. Cover and chill up to 2 hours or freeze up to 30 minutes. To serve, cook as directed. Or to reheat cooked cheese sticks that have cooled, return to air fryer and cook 30 to 60 seconds or until warm.

Valentine's Day Air Fryer Pizza

Ingredients:

- Dough
- 1 cup warm water (105-110 degrees)
- 1 tbs sugar
- 1 tbs active dry yeast
- 1 tbs olive oil
- 1 to 2 1/2 cups all purpose flour
- 1 tsp salt
- Pizza
- Dough
- Sauce
- Shredded Mozzarella Cheese
- Pepperoni
- Flour

Directions:

1. Grease the racks and set aside.
2. Put warm water into a large mixing bowl
3. Add sugar and yeast and stir to combine
4. Let mixture sit for 5 minutes, or until it becomes frothy and bubbles form.
5. Add olive oil and gently stir to combine
6. Add 2 cups of flour and salt and mix with a spatula until a ball begins to form (dough will be sticky) Add more flour as needed to form a ball. Let sit for 30 minutes.
7. Transfer to floured surface and knead into a dough, adding up to ½ cup extra flour needed.
8. Roll dough into your desired shape and gently transfer to your air fryer racks.
9. To ensure the dough doesn't form air pockets, use a fork to prick to the dough all around (gently so you don't poke holes all the way through the crust.)
10. Bake at 390 for 10 minutes, removing it half way to add pizza sauce, cheese, and pepperoni. Bake for the remaining 5 minutes.
11. Let cool, cut and serve! Enjoy!

Air Fryer Jalapeño Poppers

Servings: 4-6

Ingredients:

- 4 oz. cream cheese, at room temperature
- 2 oz. extra-sharp Cheddar, coarsely shredded (1/2 cup)
- 1 scallion, finely chopped
- Dash of hot sauce
- 6 medium to large jalapeños
- Nonstick cooking spray

Directions:

1. In medium bowl, stir to combine cream cheese, Cheddar, scallion, and hot sauce until smooth. Transfer to resealable plastic bag. Halve jalapeños lengthwise and scrape out seeds with small spoon.
2. Heat air fryer to 375°F. Snip off 1 corner of bag and pipe cheese mixture into jalapeño halves. Lightly coat air fryer basket with nonstick cooking spray and arrange poppers in single layer. Cook until tops are browned, 6 to 7 minutes.

Air Fryer Mozzarella Sticks

Servings: 24

Cooking Time: 7 Minutes

Ingredients:

- 12 sticks part-skim mozzarella string cheese*
- 3 tablespoons all-purpose flour
- 1 large egg
- 2 tablespoons nonfat milk or milk of choice
- 2/3 cup Italian-seasoned breadcrumbs whole wheat if possible
- 1/3 cup panko breadcrumbs
- 1 teaspoon Italian seasoning
- 1/4 teaspoon garlic powder
- Nonstick cooking spray or olive oil spray
- Marinara sauce or ranch dressing for serving

Directions:

1. Slice each piece of cheese in half crosswise so that you have 24 shorter pieces. Arrange the cheese in a single layer on a parchment-lined baking sheet, cutting board, or plate, then freeze until completely solid, about 1 hour.
2. Once the cheese is frozen, place the flour in a pie dish or similar shallow bowl. In a separate shallow bowl, whisk the egg and milk.
3. In a third shallow bowl, combine the Italian breadcrumbs, panko, Italian seasoning, and garlic powder. Arrange the plates in an assembly line: flour, eggs, breadcrumbs. Line a large, rimmed baking sheet with parchment paper.
4. Working to 2 to 3 cheese sticks at a time, dredge the frozen cheese sticks in the flour, shaking off excess. Next, dip into the egg, then place in the bowl with the crumbs and lightly pat to coat (don't be tempted to tackle too many cheese sticks at a time; the egg will freeze right onto the cheese and no longer be sticky enough for the crumbs to adhere).
5. Place the breaded cheese on the prepared baking sheet, then repeat the process until all of the cheese sticks are coated. Place cheese back into the freezer for at least 1 hour (this is a MUST or the cheese will melt before the crumbs are golden).
6. When ready to bake, preheat your air fryer to 390 degrees F. Generously coat the basket with nonstick spray. Arrange the frozen cheese sticks in a single layer on top, ensuring none are touching (you will need to cook them in batches). Coat the tops of the sticks with more spray.
7. Air fry mozzarella sticks for 6 to 8 minutes, until the cheese is heated through and the crumbs are golden. Remove to a plate and let stand for 3 minutes (they are HOT; you've been warned). Repeat with remaining batches. Serve warm with marinara sauce (heat the sauce first for the best experience) or ranch for dipping.

Notes

*You can also prepare this recipe with a block of mozzarella cheese rather than string cheese. Simply cut the block into 4-inch by 1/2-inch sticks.

TO MAKE AHEAD AND FREEZE: Bread the sticks as directed, then freeze until hardened. Transfer to a ziptop bag and freeze them for up to 3 months. Bake directly from frozen in the air fryer, adding to the baking time as needed.

TO STORE: Mozzarella sticks are best enjoyed immediately after making. You can try saving the leftovers in an airtight container in the refrigerator for up to 2 days.

TO REHEAT: Gently rewarm the mozzarella sticks on a baking sheet in a 350 degrees F oven until warmed through.

TO FREEZE: I recommend freezing the cheese sticks before baking if possible. If you'd like to freeze them after baking, place the mozzarella sticks on a parchment-lined baking sheet and freeze until solid. Transfer the frozen sticks to an airtight freezer-safe storage container for up to 3 months. Reheat from frozen on a baking sheet in the oven at 350 degrees F.

Air Fryer Pizza

Servings: 2
Cooking Time: 8 Minutes

Ingredients:

- olive oil cooking spray
- 1 (13.8 ounce) package refrigerated pizza dough (such as Pillsbury®)
- 6 tablespoons pizza sauce, divided
- 10 ounces shredded mozzarella cheese, divided
- 14 slices pepperoni, divided
- ½ cup onion slices, divided (Optional)
- sprinkle of dried basil and red pepper flakes (optional)

Directions:

1. Preheat the air fryer for 5 minutes at 380 degrees F (190 degrees C). Spray the air fryer basket with olive oil spray or line with a parchment liner to avoid sticking.
2. Remove crust from the can, and cut in half. Shape each piece of dough into a circle and crimping up the edges to form a crust. Make sure it'll fit in your air fryer basket. Carefully transfer one pizza crust to the air fryer basket and spray lightly with olive oil spray. Prick the dough with a fork and precook for 3 minutes.
3. Spread 3 tablespoons pizza sauce onto the crust in the air fryer basket and sprinkle with 1/2 of the mozzarella cheese. Top with 7 pepperoni slices and half of the onion slices. Sprinkle with basil and red pepper flakes, if using.
4. Cook until crust is golden brown and crispy and the cheese has melted, 7 to 9 minutes. Keep in mind that cooking times may vary depending on the brand and size of your air fryer, so check frequently to be sure nothing overcooks or burns. Repeat procedure with the second pizza crust. Serve hot.

Cook's Notes:

The easiest way to assemble the pizza is in the air fryer. It's easier to handle and ensures it'll cook through at the same time as the toppings.

I like to give the top of the pizza a little extra sprinkle of mozzarella cheese which when melted, will help anchor the toppings and keep them from flying all over the place.

If you want to keep the first pizza warm while cooking the second one, place it in the oven at the lowest temperature available. To reheat leftovers in the air fryer, set the temperature at 325 degrees F (165 degrees C), and cook for about 4 minutes.

Air Fryer Sweet Potato

Servings: 2
Cooking Time: 45 Minutes

Ingredients:

- FOR THE AIR FRYER SWEET POTATOES:
- 2 medium sweet potatoes about 8 ounces each
- 2 teaspoons extra-virgin olive oil optional
- OPTIONAL, FOR SERVING:
- Butter
- Salt and black pepper
- Chopped fresh herbs such as parsley, cilantro, or thyme
- Cinnamon and brown sugar

- Any of the variations from The Well Plated Cookbook

Directions:
1. Scrub and dry the sweet potatoes (no need to peel). Poke all over with the tines of a fork. If desired, rub the outsides of the sweet potatoes with oil. No need to wrap in foil.
2. Preheat the air fryer to 370 degrees F. Air fry the sweet potatoes until they are fork tender, about 40 to 50 minutes depending upon the size of your sweet potato.
3. Let cool a few minutes. Cut a slit in the top, then open the sweet potato and lightly fluff with a fork. Add your favorite toppings and enjoy!

Notes

TO STORE: Refrigerate sweet potatoes in an airtight storage container for up to 1 week.

TO REHEAT: Rewarm leftovers on a baking sheet in the oven at 350 degrees F or in the microwave.

TO FREEZE: Wrap sweet potatoes in plastic wrap and freeze them in an airtight freezer-safe storage container or ziptop bag for up to 3 months. Let thaw overnight in the refrigerator before reheating.

Air Fryer Tostones With Creamy Mojo Dipping Sauce

Servings: 4

Ingredients:
- 2 medium green plantains
- Olive oil cooking spray
- 3 c. warm water
- 2 1/4 tsp. kosher salt, divided, plus more
- 1/2 tsp. plus 1 pinch of garlic powder
- 1/4 c. finely chopped fresh cilantro
- 1/4 c. plain full-fat Greek yogurt
- 1 tbsp. extra-virgin olive oil
- 1 tbsp. fresh lime juice
- 1 tbsp. fresh orange juice
- 1/4 tsp. ground cumin

Directions:

1. Trim and discard ends of plantains. Using a knife, slice a slit along length of plantain peel, avoiding flesh. Slice plantain crosswise into 1" rounds. Using your fingers or back of a spoon, remove peel from each slice; discard peel.
2. Lightly coat an air-fryer basket with cooking spray. Working in batches, arrange plantains in a single layer in basket. Cook at 400° until just tender enough to smash and remain in one piece, about 6 minutes.
3. Transfer plantains to a work surface. Using bottom of a cup, flatten to a disk.
4. Meanwhile, in a large bowl, stir water, 2 teaspoons salt, and 1/2 teaspoon garlic powder until salt is dissolved. Soak tostones in water mixture 5 minutes, then pat dry with paper towels. Spray both sides of dried tostones with cooking spray.
5. Working in batches, in air-fryer basket, arrange tostones in a single layer. Cook at 400° until golden and crisp, about 7 minutes; season with salt.
6. In a small bowl, whisk cilantro, yogurt, oil, lime juice, orange juice, cumin, and remaining 1/4 tsp. salt and pinch of garlic powder until combined. Serve tostones with sauce alongside.

Air Fryer Arancini

Servings: 15

Ingredients:
- Deselect All
- 1 tablespoon olive oil
- 1 shallot, minced
- 2 cloves garlic, minced
- 1 cup arborio rice
- 1/4 cup dry white wine
- 3 cups low-sodium chicken broth, warmed
- 1/2 cup freshly grated Parmesan
- Kosher salt and freshly ground black pepper
- 1/2 cup plus 3 tablespoons Italian-style seasoned breadcrumbs
- Fifteen 1/2-inch cubes whole-milk mozzarella cheese (from a 3.5-ounce piece)

- Nonstick cooking spray, for the arancini
- Warmed marinara sauce, for serving

Directions:
1. Special equipment: a 3.5-quart air fryer
2. Heat the olive oil in a medium saucepan over medium heat. Add the shallot and garlic and cook, stirring occasionally, until tender and translucent, about 2 minutes. Add the rice and stir until lightly toasted, about 2 minutes. Pour in the wine and cook until completely absorbed, 1 to 2 minutes more. Pour in the warm chicken broth, about 1/2 cup at a time; cook, stirring constantly and allowing all of the liquid to be absorbed before adding more, until the rice is just tender, about 20 minutes. Stir in the Parmesan, 3/4 teaspoon salt and a few grinds of pepper.
3. Transfer the risotto to a shallow bowl and refrigerate until completely cool, about 1 hour and up to 8 hours (cover with plastic wrap).
4. Stir 3 tablespoons of the breadcrumbs into the risotto until evenly combined. Form the mixture into 15 arancini (each about 3 tablespoons and 1 1/2 inches in diameter). Insert 1 mozzarella cube in the center of each one, then roll between the palm of your hands to make a smooth, round ball. Refrigerate until chilled through, about 30 minutes more.
5. Preheat a 3.5-quart air fryer to 400 degrees F. Place the remaining 1/2 cup breadcrumbs in a small bowl, then roll the arancini in the breadcrumbs until evenly coated. Add the arancini to the basket and spray the tops with nonstick cooking spray. Cook until golden brown and crisp, about 10 minutes.
6. Transfer to a platter and serve with warm marinara sauce, for dipping.

Air Fryer Sausage, Peppers, And Onions

Servings: 4
Cooking Time: 20 Minutes

Ingredients:
- 4-5 Italian sausage either hot or mild
- 2 onions
- 1-2 green peppers
- 1-2 red peppers
- 1-2 yellow peppers
- 3 tablespoons olive oil
- sub roll optional, for serving

Directions:
1. Start by cutting up the peppers and onions into thin slices.
2. Then add 1 tablespoon of olive oil into each batch (I cooked them separately; if you cook them together, use less olive oil)
3. Air fry the peppers and onions for 7 minutes at 390 degrees F. I mixed them after 3 minutes.
4. Then add your sausage and air fry for 20 minutes at 390 degrees F.
5. Serve on its own or add sausage to your sub roll (I cut mine up, so they would fit nicely) and then top with onions and peppers.
6. Plate, serve, and enjoy!

Recipe Notes

This recipe can be made in the air fryer or in a skillet.

Crispy Air Fryer Pepper Rings

Servings: 4
Cooking Time: 9 Minutes

Ingredients:
- 2 large bell peppers any color
- ⅓ cup flour
- ½ teaspoon seasoned salt
- 2 eggs
- Breading
- ⅔ cup Panko bread crumbs
- ⅓ cup seasoned bread crumbs

- 2 teaspoons oil any light tasting oil

Directions:
1. Whisk eggs and salt in a small bowl (or freezer bag).
2. Combine breading ingredients in a small bowl and mix well.
3. Cut bell peppers into ½" strips and season with salt. Toss with flour.
4. Dip into the egg mixture and then into the breading mixture gently pressing to adhere.
5. Preheat air fryer to 400°F.
6. Place peppers in a single layer in the basket. Cook 9-11 minutes or until golden. Repeat with remaining vegetables.

Reheat Pizza In The Air Fryer

Servings: 1
Cooking Time: 3 Minutes

Ingredients:
- 1-2 leftover pizza slices

Directions:
1. Preheat air fryer to 350 degrees.
2. Place pizza slice(s) inside the air fryer in one single layer and cook for 3-4 minutes.*
3. Remove leftover pizza from the air fryer and enjoy!

NOTES
* if pizza is not thoroughly reheated, continue to cook in increments of 1-2 minutes.

THICK CRUST PIZZA
Thicker pizza crusts need an extra minute or two to warm up.

THIN CRUST PIZZA
Air fry thin-crust pizza at up to 400 degrees for just 2 minutes.

DEEP DISH PIZZA
Air fry deep dish pizza at 330 degrees for about 6 minutes.

Burst Tomato Cottage Cheese Caprese Bowl

Servings: 1
Cooking Time: 5 Minutes

Ingredients:
- 1 cup Good Culture cottage cheese (I used whole, you can use 2%)
- 1 cup grape tomatoes
- 2 teaspoons extra virgin olive oil
- 1 teaspoon balsamic glaze
- fresh basil (for garnish)
- pinch kosher salt
- black pepper to taste

Directions:
1. Season tomatoes in a medium bowl with 1 teaspoon olive oil and pinch of salt. Air fry 400F 5 to 6 minutes, shaking the basket halfway, until they burst.
2. Place cottage cheese in a bowl, top with tomatoes, drizzle more oil, balsamic glaze, salt, pepper, and garnish with basil.

Air Fryer Hot Dogs

Servings: 4
Cooking Time: 5 Minutes

Ingredients:
- 4 hot dogs (or as many hot dogs as your air fryer basket fits)
- 4 hot dog buns, sliced down the middle (optional)

Directions:
1. Preheat air fryer to 400 degrees.
2. Cook hot dogs for 4 minutes until cooked, flipping the hot dogs halfway through cooking.
3. Place hot dogs into hot dog buns.
4. Cook hot dogs in buns an additional 1-2 minutes, still at 400 degrees.
5. Enjoy immediately.

NOTES
To air fry frozen hot dogs:
Preheat air fryer to 350 degrees

Microwave hot dogs for 30 seconds - 1 minute on defrost (optional)

Cook on 350 for 7-8 minutes until hot dog is heated thoroughly

Air Fryer Crescent Mummy Dogs

Servings: 10

Ingredients:

- 1 can (8 oz) refrigerated Pillsbury™ Original Crescent Rolls (8 Count)
- 2 1/2 slices American cheese (2.5 oz)
- 10 hot dogs
- Mustard or ketchup, if desired

Directions:

1. Cut 8-inch round of cooking parchment paper. Place in bottom of air fryer basket.
2. Unroll dough; separate at perforations, creating 4 rectangles. Press perforations to seal.
3. With knife or kitchen scissors, cut each rectangle lengthwise into 10 pieces, making a total of 40 pieces of dough. Cut cheese slices lengthwise into quarters (1/2 slice cheese, cut in half).
4. Wrap 4 pieces of dough around each hot dog and 1/4 slice of cheese to look like "bandages," stretching dough slightly to completely cover hot dog. About 1/2 inch from one end of each hot dog, separate "bandages" so hot dog shows through for "face." Place 3 to 4 crescent dogs (cheese side down) on parchment in air fryer basket, spacing apart.
5. Set air fryer to 325°F; cook 6 to 7 minutes or until crescent tops are light brown. With tongs, turn over each one; cook 2 to 3 minutes or until golden brown. Remove from air fryer. Repeat with remaining crescent dogs.
6. With mustard, draw features on "face." Serve warm.

Hawaiian Pizza

Ingredients:

- 11 oz. Pre-made pizza dough
- 5 Tbsp. Pizza sauce
- 1 cup Mozzarella cheese
- 1/2 cup cooked ham or Canadian Bacon
- 1/2 cup Pineapple Chunks

Directions:

1. Spread marinara sauce on the pre-made dough. If you like crust, leave a little bread showing on the edges.
2. Sprinkle the mozzarella cheese on top of the marinara.
3. Add the ham & pineapple.
4. Place in the air fryer at 420 for 15 minutes or until cheese and veggies have fully cooked.
5. Plate, serve, and enjoy!

Air Fryer Fried Rice

Servings: 4

Cooking Time: 15 Minutes

Ingredients:

- 3 c rice cooked and cold
- 1 c frozen vegetables I used carrot, corn, broccoli and edamame
- 1/3 c coconut aminos
- 1 T oil
- 2 eggs scrambled (optional)

Directions:

1. To make your air fryer fried rice, put your cold rice into an large bowl.
2. Then add your frozen vegetables to the rice bowl.
3. If you are using egg or another protein, add it to the rice bowl now.
4. Next up, you are going to add the coconut aminos and oil to your bowl.
5. Mix, mix, mix until well combined. Then transfer to the rice mixture to an oven safe container.
6. Place that container into your air fryer. Cook the air fryer fried rice at 360 degrees F for 15 minutes.

I would suggest stirring 3 times through the 15 minutes.
7. Enjoy!

Notes

Tips for Air Fryer Fried Rice:

Add in whatever protein you like: eggs, tofu, chicken, turkey

Be sure to stir the air fryer fried rice several times within the 15 minute cooking period. This helps it cook evenly.

If you are gluten-free be sure to check the soy sauce if you are using that. Coconut Aminos is my gluten-free go to when it comes to a soy sauce flavor.

Use any combinations of frozen veggies that you like.

Mummy Hotdogs

Ingredients:

- 1 can crescent dough rolls
- 10 hot dogs
- 3 slices American Cheese
- Mustard or ketchup

Directions:

1. Unroll crescent dough, separate at perforations, making a large rectangle. Press perforations to seal so there are no holes.
2. With pizza cutter, cut the dough lengthwise about ½ inch thick, and same for the cheese.
3. Place a sliver of cheese lengthwise on the hotdog. Stretch the dough slightly and wrap around the hotdog. About ½ inch from the top of the hotdog, separate the "bandages" to leave room for a face.
4. Place wrapped hotdogs into the air fryer, not touching each other.
5. Bake at 390 for 10 minutes or until dough is golden-brown.

Latin Yellow Rice

Servings: 8
Cooking Time: 25 Minutes

Ingredients:

- 2 cups uncooked long grain rice
- 4 teaspoon olive oil
- 1 large chicken or veggie bouillon cube (such as knorrs or maggi)
- 5 medium scallions (chopped)
- 2 garlic cloves (minced)
- 1 medium tomato (diced)
- 1/2 cup chopped cilantro
- 4 cups water
- 1 packet Badia Sazon seasoning
- 1 teaspoon kosher salt (or more to taste)

Directions:

1. In a medium heavy pot with a tight fitting lid, heat oil on medium heat and saute scallions, cilantro and garlic for about 2 minutes, until tender,
2. Add the tomatoes and saute another minute, until they get soft.
3. Add rice and saute 2 minutes longer, stirring frequently.
4. Add water, bouillon cube, sazón plus 1 teaspoon salt.
5. Taste 4 cups water and taste for salt, it should be flavorful and salty enough, adjust as needed.
6. Let the water boil on a high heat stirring once at this point.
7. As the water boils down and just barely skims the top of the rice, reduce heat to very low and cover 15 minutes.
8. The steam will cook the rice so do not open the lid.
9. After 15 minutes, shut the flame off and let it sit at least 5 more minutes without touching the lid.
10. The steam will finish cooking the rice without burning the bottom. Then fluff with a fork and enjoy.

Notes

*Badia makes a sazon that contains no msg.
Helpful Tips:

Water to rice ratio – I use long grain rice and keep the water to rice ratio 2 to 1. If you use short grain rice, you may want to reduce the liquid to 1.5 to 1.

To rinse the rice or not – I never rinse my rice, but many people do. Rinsing it does make it less starchy. Whether you rinse it or not it will still turn out fine.

Don't touch until it's done. Let it sit 5 minutes after cooking, then fluff the rice with a fork. Don't stir it while it's cooking, it will smash the rice.

Don't open the lid until it's finished and has rested 5 minutes. The steam is what will finish cooking the rice, if you lift the lid you will lose the steam.

You will need a heavy pot with a tight fitted lid to make rice. This is a must, if any steam escapes your rice will be under cooked.

If you don't have a tight fitted lid, you can place a sheet of foil over the pot, then top with the lid to prevent steam from escaping.

Don't cover the rice until most of the liquid has been absorbed and is just skimming the top or it will come out too wet.

Air Fryer Smoked Sausage

Servings: 4
Cooking Time: 8 Minutes

Ingredients:

- 12 ounces smoked sausage
- 2 tablespoons bbq sauce optional

Directions:

1. Preheat the air fryer to 400°F.
2. Cut sausage into ½" slices and toss with bbq sauce if using and place in the air fryer basket.
3. Cook for 7-8 minutes shaking the basket halfway through cooking.
4. Serve with bbq sauce or dijon mustard.

Notes

Any smoked sausage will work in this recipe.
For best results, preheat the air fryer.
Don't overcrowd the air fryer.
Appliances can vary, check the sausage a couple of minutes early so they don't burn.

Air Fryer Wonton Mozzarella Sticks

Servings: 6
Cooking Time: 6 Minutes

Ingredients:

- 6 mozzarella cheese sticks
- 6 egg roll wrappers
- olive oil cooking spray
- kosher salt

Directions:

1. Place a piece of string cheese near the bottom corner of the egg roll wrapper. Roll up halfway and carefully fold the sides toward the center over the cheese. Dip your finger in water and trace the edges of the wrapper. Roll the remaining wrapper around the mozzarella stick. Repeat with remaining wrappers and cheese.
2. Place six of the mozzarella sticks in a single layer in the air fryer basket and spray with olive oil spray. Sprinkle with kosher salt.
3. Air fry at 350 degrees for 3 minutes, flip, spray the other side with olive oil spray and sprinkle with kosher salt, then continue cooking for another 3 minutes until they are crisp and golden brown. Serve with a marinara sauce or your choice of dipping sauces, if desired.

NOTES

Mozzarella sticks should not touch each other when air frying.

Make sure your string cheese is cold, not room temperature when making this recipe.

If your cheese completely oozed out of your mozzarella stick during the cooking time, you either (1) cooked them too long, (2) didn't seal the corners and edges with water well enough, or (3) didn't use cold mozzarella cheese. The wrapper should have no cracks or holes. A small amount of cheese oozing from the end of the mozzarella stick is normal, but not all of the cheese should melt out. The mozzarella cheese should be just melted and the wrapper will be crispy on the edges and slightly chewy towards the middle.

Air Fryer Frozen Pizza

Servings: 1
Cooking Time: 8 Minutes

Ingredients:

- 1 Frozen Pizza

Directions:

1. Open packing and place pizza in the air fryer basket.
2. Air fry at 380 degrees F for 6-8 minutes, until crispy.

SNACKS & APPETIZERS RECIPES

Air Fryer Snap Peas

Servings: 4

Cooking Time: 6 Minutes

Ingredients:
- 2 cups snap peas fresh
- 1 tablespoon sesame oil
- 1 teaspoon minced garlic
- 1/2 teapsoon kosher salt

Directions:
1. Rinse snap peas under cool water and pat them dry completely with paper towels. Trim ends and then place snap peas in a medium-sized bowl.
2. Measure and pour sesame oil, garlic, and salt over snap peas. Toss peas in bowl with oil mixture until they are fully coated.
3. Transfer peas to the air fryer basket, spreading them out in a single layer so they don't overlap and can cook evenly.
4. Air Fry at 380 degrees F for 6-8 minutes. Serve when finished cooking.

NOTES

Optional Flavors: Adding extra seasonings can really change up this side dish. For extra flavors, add a pinch of black pepper, chili powder, a tablespoon soy sauce, red pepper flakes, Cajun seasoning, lemon juice, garlic powder, blackening seasoning or parmesan cheese.

Optional Toppings: You can top these peas with pickled onions, crumbled bacon bits, diced peppers, scallions, chop walnuts, pumpkin seeds or almonds into pieces. Black or toasted sesame seeds will also add extra crunch.

Optional Favorite Dipping Sauce: Any favorite dipping sauce such as teriyaki sauce, Greek yogurt with a bit of spice, garlic hummus, mustard sauce or hot chili sauce, are all perfect for dipping.

Cooking Tips: These are super tasty at room temperature, warm or hot. To ensure they are super crispy spritz basket with olive oil spray prior to cooking.

Substitutions: If you do not have sesame oil use a tablespoon olive oil.

Air Fryer Sweet Potato Wedges

Servings: 4

Cooking Time: 20 Minutes

Ingredients:
- 4 large sweet potatoes*
- 1 tbsp oil (I used olive oil)
- 1 tsp smoked paprika
- 1 tsp garlic powder
- Salt and pepper according to taste

Directions:
1. Preheat the air fryer to 200C/190F.
2. Prepare the sweet potatoes by chopping off the ends and cleaning them. Slice them lengthwise into similar-sized wedges.
3. Drizzle with oil and add seasoning. Toss the sweet potato wedges in the oil and seasoning, ensuring they are all coated.
4. Transfer to the air fryer basket and set the timer for 20 minutes. Check on them at the halfway mark to shake them about.
5. After 20 minutes, they should be crispy on the outside and soft and fluffy on the inside. If they are not, return them to the air fryer and continue cooking, checking on them after 2 minutes.
6. Serve the sweet potato wedges as a side dish or with your favourite dip.

Notes

*Sweet Potatoes: if you don't have large sweet potatoes use 2 or 3 mediums ones.

Air-fryer Haloumi Popcorn With Maple Hot Sauce

Servings: 40
Cooking Time: 10 Minutes

Ingredients:
- 2 tsp smoked paprika
- 1 tsp brown sugar
- 1 tsp KEEN'S Mustard Powder
- 1 tsp cornflour
- 1 tsp onion powder
- 1/2 tsp garlic powder
- 225g haloumi, cut into 1cm pieces
- 2 eggs
- 60g (1 1/4 cups) panko breadcrumbs
- 1 tbsp finely chopped fresh thyme leaves, plus extra, to serve (optional)
- Maple hot sauce
- 1 tbsp maple syrup
- 1 tbsp sriracha chilli sauce
- 1 1/2 tsp apple cider vinegar
- Select all ingredients

Directions:
1. Preheat an air fryer to 180C. Line a large baking tray with baking paper.
2. Combine the paprika, sugar, mustard powder, cornflour, onion powder and garlic powder in a medium shallow dish. Add the haloumi, a few pieces at a time, and stir to coat. Transfer to the prepared tray.
3. Whisk the eggs in another medium shallow dish. Add the coated haloumi, a few pieces at a time, and stir to coat. Return pieces to the tray.
4. Combine the breadcrumbs and thyme in another medium shallow dish. Add the haloumi, a few pieces a time, and turn to coat. Return pieces to the tray. Place in the freezer for 5 minutes to chill.
5. Meanwhile, to make the maple hot sauce, place all ingredients in a small serving bowl and whisk to combine.
6. Place the crumbed haloumi pieces in the air fryer and fry for 6-8 minutes or until the crust is golden and the cheese is soft. Transfer to a serving plate. Sprinkle with extra thyme and drizzle over a little maple hot sauce. Serve with remaining sauce.

Air-fryer Scallops With Lemon-herb Sauce

Servings: 2

Ingredients:
- 8 large (1-oz.) sea scallops, cleaned and patted very dry
- ¼ teaspoon ground pepper
- ⅛ teaspoon salt
- cooking spray
- ¼ cup extra-virgin olive oil
- 2 tablespoon very finely chopped flat-leaf parsley
- 2 teaspoon capers, very finely chopped
- 1 teaspoon finely grated lemon zest
- ½ teaspoon finely chopped garlic
- lemon wedges, optional

Directions:
1. Sprinkle scallops with pepper and salt. Coat the basket of an air fryer with cooking spray. Place scallops in the basket and coat them with cooking spray. Place the basket in the fryer. Cook the scallops at 400°F until they reach an internal temperature of 120°F, about 6 minutes.
2. Combine oil, parsley, capers, lemon zest and garlic in a small bowl. Drizzle over the scallops. Serve with lemon wedges, if desired.

Kids' Air-fryer Chickpea, Zucchini & Spinach Nuggets

Servings: 4
Cooking Time: 50 Minutes

Ingredients:

- 1 zucchini, coarsely chopped
- 45g baby spinach leaves
- 840g canned Woolworths no-added-salt chickpeas, rinsed, drained
- 2 tbs plain flour
- 1 tbs dried Italian herbs
- 1 cup panko breadcrumbs
- 5ml olive oil cooking spray
- 200g Solanato tomatoes, halved (to serve)
- 60g mixed salad leaves (to serve)
- Veggie tomato sauce
- 140g no-added-salt tomato paste
- 1 carrot, grated
- 1 zucchini, grated
- 400g canned Woolworths no-added-salt diced tomatoes

Directions:

1. Place zucchini, spinach, chickpeas, flour and herbs in a food processor and process for 30 seconds or until smooth. Season with pepper.
2. Shape 1 1/2 tablespoonfuls of mixture into 24 nuggets. Place breadcrumbs in a shallow bowl. Coat nuggets, one at a time, in breadcrumbs, then transfer to a baking paper-lined tray. Spray tops of nuggets with oil.
3. Preheat air fryer to 200°C. Spray air-fryer basket with oil. Place 8 nuggets, oiledsides down, in a single layer in basket. Spray nuggets with oil. Cook for 16 minutes or until golden. Repeat with remaining nuggets and oil.
4. Meanwhile, to make the veggie tomato sauce, place all the ingredients in a small saucepan over medium heat. Cook, stirring, for 3 minutes or until vegetables have softened. Season with pepper. Transfer to a food processor and process for 10 seconds or until smooth.
5. Toss tomato and salad leaves in a bowl. Serve nuggets with veggie tomato sauce and salad.

Air Fryer Breaded Asparagus Fries

Servings: 2
Cooking Time: 10 Minutes

Ingredients:

- 1/2 pound (227 g) fresh asparagus, ends trimmed
- 1 (1) egg, beaten
- 1/4 teaspoon (1.25 ml) salt, or to taste
- black pepper, to taste
- 1/2 teaspoon (2.5 ml) garlic powder, or to taste
- 1/4 cup (27 g) bread crumbs (Italian style or Japanese panko)
- 2 Tablespoons (30 ml) grated parmesan cheese
- Oil spray, for coating asparagus fries
- Dips: hot sauce, ranch, bbq sauce, etc (optional)
- EQUIPMENT
- Air Fryer
- Oil Sprayer

Directions:

1. Pre-heat air fryer at 380°F/193°C for 5 minutes.
2. Trim the tough bottom ends of the asparagus (usually about the bottom 1-2 inches).
3. Lay the asparagus out on a board or plate and brush with the beaten egg. Season to taste with salt, pepper and garlic powder evenly over asparagus. Gently toss to coat evenly.
4. On a plate combine the bread crumbs and parmesan cheese. Toss seasoned asparagus in the bread crumb/parmesan mix, gently shaking off any excess coating.
5. Spray all sides of the breaded asparagus with oil spray. Dry breading might fly around in air fryer and burn, so make sure to coat any dry spots.
6. Spray air fryer basket/tray and place asparagus in the air fryer in a single layer.
7. Air Fry at 380°F/193°C for 5-8 minutes. Gently flip and spray any remaining dry spots with oil spray.

8. Air Fry at 380°F/193°C for additional 3-5 minutes or until crispy golden brown. Serve warm with your favorite dip.

Air Fryer Asparagus Fries

Servings: 4
Cooking Time: 8 Minutes

Ingredients:
- 1 pound asparagus
- 2 eggs
- 1 cup panko breadcrumbs
- 1 teaspoon garlic powder
- 1/2 teaspoon smoked paprika
- 1 teaspoon ground black pepper
- 1/2 teaspoon olive oil cooking spray

Directions:
1. Rinse the asparagus in cold water then pat the fresh asparagus spears dry with a paper towel.
2. Trim the ends of the asparagus (approximately 2 inches) with a sharp kitchen knife and set aside.
3. Whisk the eggs together in a shallow bowl.
4. In a separate bowl, combine the panko breadcrumbs, garlic powder, smoked paprika and ground black pepper.
5. Then pour the breadcrumb mixture into a second shallow dish.
6. Dip asparagus spears in the egg mixture, then dip each spear into the breadcrumb coating. Make sure you have a full uniform coating on each spear.
7. Spray each asparagus with cooking spray (olive oil).
8. Place the breaded spears in a single layer into the air fryer basket.
9. Air fry asparagus fries at 400 degrees F for 7-8 minutes, use a pair of tongs and flip the asparagus halfway through the cooking process.
10. Carefully remove them from the air fryer basket and place them on a baking sheet with parchment paper to fully cool if making more than one batch.
11. Serve while hot.

NOTES

Optional Favorite Dipping Sauce: blue cheese dressing, hot sauce mixed with Greek yogurt, whole grain mustard, basil lemon dipping sauce or try a gooey hot cheese mixture.

Aioli Ingredients: Making an aioli from scratch requires 1 cup mayonnaise and any desired spices or flavors that you and your family enjoy.

Kitchen Tips: Use the asparagus trimmings to flavor soups, stews or in pasta water to add extra flavor. Use a food processor to mix dry ingredients if you prefer.

Substitutions: Use non-stick spray, refined coconut oil instead of olive oil spray. If you do not have panko, use 1 cup Italian-style breadcrumbs or a panko cheese mixture with plain bread crumbs. Almond flour mixture and coconut flour with grated cheese can replace the breadcrumbs.

I make this recipe in my 5.8 qt. Cosori air fryer. Depending on your air fryer, size and wattages, the cooking time may need to be adjusted 1-2 minutes.

Perfect Hot Chips

Servings: 4
Cooking Time: 15 Minutes

Ingredients:
- Perfect hot chips
- 8 desiree or king edward potatoes, peeled
- rice bran or peanut oil, to deep-fry
- tomato or barbecue sauce or vinegar, to serve (optional)
- salt

Directions:
1. Perfect hot chips
2. Cut potatoes lengthways into 1cm-wide strips. Set aside in a bowl of iced water until ready to cook. Drain and dry thoroughly.
3. Heat oil in saucepan to 160°C, or test by dipping a chip into oil - if bubbles appear instantly, oil is hot enough. Using a wire basket, perforated spoon or wire skimmer, lower chips in batches into oil and cook for 8 minutes, until tender but not brown. Remove from oil and drain on paper towel.

4. Reheat oil to 185°C. Gently lower chips into oil briefly, until crisp and brown. Drain on paper towel, sprinkle with salt and serve immediately with your choice of condiments.

Notes

A mandolin makes uniform slices that will cook evenly.

Air Fryer Kale Chips

Servings: 4
Cooking Time: 24 Minutes

Ingredients:

- ½ bunch of Kale
- 2 tablespoon of olive oil
- 1 tablespoon of nutritional yeast
- ¼ teaspoon of sea salt
- ⅛ teaspoon of pepper

Directions:

1. Wash your kale leaves and lie to dry on paper towels, or spin dry them if you have a salad spinner. Begin by laying your kale leaf on a cutting board and cutting down the sides of the stalk. Then discard the stalk. Take the two leaves and tear them into smaller pieces.
2. Place them in a bowl and drizzle olive oil over your kale, and using your hands, massage the oil evenly onto all of the kale pieces.
3. Sprinkle the nutritional yeast, salt, and pepper and toss to coat.
4. Preheat your air fryer to 270 degrees.
5. Place your kale in the basket, in as close to a single layer as possible. You will be cooking in batches. Cook for 5-7 minutes, tossing the kale chips every 3 minutes to prevent burnt chips.

Air Fryer Fried Ravioli

Servings: 8
Cooking Time: 8 Minutes

Ingredients:

- 1 cup Italian Breadcrumbs
- 1/4 cup Parmesan cheese, finely shredded
- 2 teaspoons dried basil
- 1/2 teaspoon ground black pepper
- 1/2 teaspoon garlic powder
- 2 large eggs whisked
- 1/2 cup all purpose flour
- 18 Ravioli frozen, cheese
- 2 teaspoons olive oil to spray tops of breaded ravioli

Directions:

1. Preheat the air fryer to 350 degrees Fahrenheit.
2. In a shallow dish, mix breadcrumbs, parmesan cheese, dried basil, black pepper, and garlic powder together.
3. Measure and pour flour into a medium bowl.
4. Crack eggs and whisk in a separate bowl.
5. Dip ravioli in flour to coat both sides and shake off excess.
6. Next dip the ravioli in the egg mixture, then the breadcrumb mixture, patting crumbs into the ravioli so that it adheres.
7. In batches, arrange ravioli in a single layer in the air fryer basket.
8. Spray each ravioli with cooking spray.
9. Air fry ravioli at 350 degrees F for 7-8 minutes, flipping halfway through the cooking process until golden brown.

NOTES

Optional Toppings: Fresh minced basil, a dusting of parmesan cheese,

Optional Favorite Dipping Sauces: Warm marinara sauce, ranch dressing, alfredo sauce, red pepper flakes with sour cream, gooey cheese sauce with fresh herbs.

Substitutions: Cheese ravioli, panko breadcrumbs, pumpkin ravioli, mushroom ravioli, seasoned breadcrumbs,

I make this recipe in my Cosori 5.8 qt. air fryer. Depending on your air fryer, size, and wattages cook time may need to be adjusted 1-2 minutes.

Air Fryer Pickle Poppers

Servings: 6
Cooking Time: 10 Minutes

Ingredients:
- 6 medium dill pickles
- 4 ounces cream cheese softened
- 1/4 cup cheddar cheese shredded
- 12 slices bacon

Directions:
1. Cut the pickles in half, lengthwise on a cutting board, then use a spoon to scoop out the center of pickles to create a trench for the cream cheese.
2. Cut small slices of the cream cheese, in thin strips, and place a strip inside each cored pickle half, then top with a sprinkle of cheddar cheese.
3. Wrap a piece of bacon around the stuffed pickle slice and secure with a toothpick.
4. Place the pickles in the basket of the air fryer in a single layer. Be sure they aren't overlapping each other in the basket.
5. Air fry at 370 degrees F for 10-12 minutes, until the bacon is cooked to your desired crispness and is golden brown.

NOTES
Optional Favorite Dipping Sauce: Sour cream, chives with pickle juice, spicy ranch dressing, blue cheese dressing, greek yogurt with chopped parsley, honey mustard sauce or a cheesy garlic sauce.
Kitchen Tips: I would recommend making a double batch because these are so good.

Air Fryer Nachos

Servings: 2
Cooking Time: 3 Minutes

Ingredients:
- 2 cups tortilla chips
- 2 cups shredded cheddar cheese
- 1 tomato small and diced
- ¼ cup black olives
- 1 jalapeno small and diced
- Optional Toppings:
- 1 cup meat hamburger meat, or fajita steak strips
- black or refried beans
- green onions
- sour cream
- salsa

Directions:
1. Line the air fryer basket with a sheet of aluminum foil. Leave about 2-3 inches on two sides for easy lifting of nachos when done air frying.
2. Once the basket is lined, add chips, and spread out in the basket.
3. Evenly top tortilla chips with cheese, tomatoes, olives, and the jalapenos. Air fry at 320 degrees for 3-5 minutes until the cheese is melted.
4. Carefully lift the nachos from the basket using the extra inches of foil. Top with favorite nacho toppings such as avocado, sour cream, green onions, cilantro, or salsa.

Sweet Potato Fries With An Air Fryer

Ingredients:
- 2 sweet potatoes
- 1 tbsp olive or avocado oil
- ½ tsp salt

Directions:
1. Peel and slice the potatoes into French Fry sized slices. Place in a large bowl coat with oil and salt. Then place potatoes into the air fryer basket, forming an even layer. Cook at 400-degree for 5 minutes. Then remove the air fryer basket. Shake the basket to turn the potatoes for even cooking continue to air fry for an additional 15 minutes. Continue to shake up the fries every 5 minutes and check for doneness. Cooking time may vary depending on the size of the potato slices.
2. Some GoWISE USA air fryers include a Fries/Chips program, pre-set with the time and temperature.

Salt & Pepper Chilli Chips

Servings: 4

Ingredients:

- 600g potatoes, cut into chips about 1cm thickness
- 1/2 red pepper thinly sliced
- 1-2 red chillis, sliced
- 1 garlic clove crushed
- 2 spring onion, sliced into 2cm strips
- 1/2 white onion thinly sliced
- 1 tbsp cooking oil
- Seasoning (you can increase the measurements and batch prep this for future use
- 1 tsp fine salt
- 1/4 tsp chilli powder
- 1 tsp white pepper
- 1 tsp Chinese 5 spice
- 1/4 tsp msg(optional) if using cut the salt to 1/2 tsp
- COOKING MODE
- When entering cooking mode - We will enable your screen to stay 'always on' to avoid any unnecessary interruptions whilst you cook!

Directions:

1. Soak your chips in water for at least 30 mins, drain and pat dry them. Season with salt pepper and drizzle with oil, mixing well. Cook in your Air-fryer for 20 mins at 200°C until golden brown and crispy.
2. In the mean time, heat a wok or a sauté pan and fry off the white onions for 1 minute, then add the peppers, fry off the for another minute and add the spring onions and garlic.
3. Add the chips and toss the wok to mix well, season with salt and pepper seasoning and mix everything again.
4. Serve as a side with your favourite fakeaway.

Air Fryer Zucchini Chips Recipe

Servings: 4

Cooking Time: 10 Minutes

Ingredients:

- 1 medium Zucchini
- 1 tbsp Olive oil
- 1/4 tsp Sea salt
- 1/8 tsp Black pepper

Directions:

1. Use a mandoline to slice zucchini into 1/8 in (0.3 cm) thick slices.
2. Pat any excess liquid off of the zucchini slices with a paper towel.
3. Preheat air fryer to 325 degrees F (162 degrees C).
4. In a medium bowl, combine the zucchini slices, olive oil, sea salt and pepper. Toss until all slices are coated.
5. Place the zucchini slices in a single layer in the air fryer. Cook for 8-12 minutes. Check at the 8 minute mark and remove any slices that are browning/crisping. Continue to check every couple of minutes until all slices are done. Repeat with all zucchini slices. Zucchini will crisp up a more while cooling.

Banana Chips

Servings: 3-4

Cooking Time: 1 To 2 Hours

Ingredients:

- 2–3 large, almost ripe bananas, peeled and thinly sliced (3mm/no more than ⅛in thick) on a sharp diagonal
- light rapeseed, vegetable or sunflower oil
- 1 lemon, juice only
- ground cinnamon (optional)

Directions:

1. Preheat the oven to 120C/100C Fan/Gas ½. Line a large baking sheet with baking paper and brush all over very lightly with oil.

2. Put the banana slices into a bowl, drizzle over the lemon juice and gently stir to coat.
3. Lift the banana slices from the juice and place on the baking sheet in a single layer. Sprinkle over a few pinches of cinnamon if you like, then bake for 1 hour.
4. Carefully peel the slices from the paper, turn over and bake for a further 30–40 minutes. The slices should feel dry on both sides – they'll crisp up some more as they cool.
5. Leave to cool completely before serving or storing in an airtight container.

NOTES

As a snack for adults, sprinkle with a little salt.

To air-fry, coat the banana slices in lemon juice as above. Lightly oil or oil-spray the air fryer basket. Add some banana slices in a single layer, then air-fry at 100C for 20 minutes. Carefully turn and rotate the slices and continue to cook for 5 minutes at a time, removing them as they feel crisp and dried out (remove any that have browned too much even if they don't feel crisp – they will crisp more as they cool). Repeat until all the banana slices are crisp – this should take no more than 30 minutes.

Air Fryer Frozen Tater Tots

Servings: 4
Cooking Time: 9 Minutes

Ingredients:
- 1 lb. (454 g) Frozen Tater Tots (Potato Puffs, etc.)
- salt , to taste
- black pepper , to taste
- optional dipping sauce (ketchup, bbq sauce, mustard, ranch, hot sauce, queso, etc.)
- EQUIPMENT
- Air Fryer

Directions:
1. Place the frozen tots (puffs)in the air fryer basket and spread out evenly. No oil spray is needed.
2. Air Fry at 400°F/205°C for 5-8 minutes. Shake and gently stir about halfway through cooking. If cooking larger batches, or if your tots (puffs) don't cook evenly, try turning them multiple times on following batches.
3. If needed air fry at 400°F/205°C for an additional 1-3 minutes or until crisped to your liking. Season with salt & pepper if desired and serve with optional dipping sauce.

NOTES

Air Frying Tips and Notes:

No Oil Necessary. Cook Frozen - Do not thaw first.

Shake or turn if needed. Don't overcrowd the air fryer basket.

Recipe timing is based on a non-preheated air fryer. If cooking in multiple batches back to back, the following batches may cook a little quicker.

Recipes were tested in 3.7 to 6 qt. air fryers. If using a larger air fryer, they might cook quicker so adjust cooking time.

Remember to set a timer to shake/flip/toss as directed in recipe.

Air Fryer Chips

Servings: 3-5
Cooking Time: 25 Minutes

Ingredients:
- 600g potatoes
- Oil (optional)
- Seasoning

Directions:
1. Slice the potatoes up - thick for regular chips, or thin for French fries. You can either peel the potatoes, or give them a good scrub and leave the skin on.
2. Preheat air fryer to 200C/400F
3. Wash them in cold water to remove the starch.
4. Pat dry with kitchen towel or a tea towel.
5. Optionally spray with some oil.
6. Sprinkle with seasoning of your choice (chip seasoning, curry powder, paprika, salt and pepper).
7. Transfer to the air fryer basket.

8. Cook for 20 to 25 minutes, checking regularly and shaking/turning. Depending on the thickness of the chip, or how crispy you like them, you might want to cook them for longer.

Air Fryer Tater Tots

Servings: 4
Cooking Time: 10 Minutes

Ingredients:
- 35-40 frozen tater tots
- 2 teaspoons canola oil
- ½ teaspoon seasoning salt

Directions:
1. Preheat air fryer to 375 for 5 minutes.
2. Open air fryer and brush basket with 1 teaspoon oil.
3. Arrange tater tots in a single layer on the rack. Brush with remaining oil and sprinkle with seasoning salt.
4. Cook at 375 degrees F for 7-8 minutes. Open air fryer and flip (if desired, to brown the other side). Cook an additional 5 minutes or until cooked to desired doneness.

Dirty Fries

Servings: 2
Cooking Time: 45 Minutes

Ingredients:
- 3 large potatoes
- 4 bacon medallions diced
- 80 g low fat cheese
- 2 peppers, red and green diced
- 1 onion diced
- 3 spring onions
- 2 tsp Cajun seasoning
- 1 tbsp Worcestershire sauce
- 1 pinch sea salt
- low calorie cooking spray

Directions:
1. ACTIFRY Directions:
2. Cut the potatoes into chips. You don't have to peel them but make sure you wash them. Toss them in a decent amount of low calorie cooking spray, 1 tsp of the Cajun spice mix, and then season them well.
3. Cook for 30 minutes in the Actifry, then set them aside.
4. Add the onions, peppers, bacon, remaining Cajun seasoning and Worcestershire sauce to the air fryer. Spray with some low calorie cooking spray and cook for 10 minutes.
5. Return the chips and cook for 1 minute, then remove the paddle and sprinkle the cheese over the top of the chips.
6. Cook for 1 minute and serve.
7. OVEN Directions:
8. Pre heat the oven to 200°C. Then cut the potatoes into chips. There's no need to peel them.
9. Place them in a pan of boiling salted water and simmer until they start to soften but are still quite firm.
10. Drain the potatoes and spray a baking tray with low calorie cooking spray. Coat the potatoes in low calorie cooking spray and sprinkle them with a little salt and half of the Cajun seasoning.
11. Place in the oven for 20-30 minutes until they are soft and starting to colour.
12. Meanwhile, spray a frying pan with a generous amount of low calorie cooking spray, then add the chopped peppers, bacon, onions, Worcestershire sauce and remaining Cajun seasoning.
13. Cook for a few minutes until they start to soften. When the chips are cooked and browned, add them to the frying pan and stir well.
14. Place the contents into an oven proof dish and cook in the oven for 5-10 minutes, or until the cheese has melted. Then serve.

Crispy Air Fryer Dill Pickles

Servings: 6
Cooking Time: 10 Minutes

Ingredients:
- 16 Pickle Spears
- 1/2 cup all purpose flour
- 2 large eggs
- 1 Tablespoon water
- 1/4 teaspoon hot sauce such as Tabasco
- 1 1/2 cups panko breadcrumbs
- 1/2 teaspoon ground black pepper
- 1/2 teaspoon dried dill
- 1 teaspoon olive oil cooking spray

Directions:
1. Preheat the air fryer to 400 degrees Fahrenheit.
2. Drain pickles in a strainer and pat them dry with paper towels to remove the excess juice.
3. In a small bowl add flour.
4. Use a second bowl to whisk eggs, water and hot sauce together.
5. In a medium bowl combine the bread crumbs, black pepper and dried dill.
6. Dredge the pickles in the flour mixture (shake off any excess flour), then dip into the egg mixture and lastly into the breadcrumbs. Coated pickle slices should be covered evenly.
7. Spray each pickle with cooking spray and place them in the air fryer basket in a single layer.
8. Cook for 5 minutes, flip and cook for an additional 4-6 minutes or until crispy and golden brown.

NOTES

I make this recipe in my Cosori 5.8 qt. air fryer. Depending on your air fryer, size and wattages, cook times may need to be adjusted 1-2 minutes.

Optional Additional Seasonings: Change up the flavors by adding garlic powder, chipotle pepper, Italian seasoning, cayenne pepper, kosher salt, and parmesan cheese.

Substitutions: You can use almond flour or coconut flour as a substitute for all-purpose flour. They will be just as tasty. You can also use extra panko breadcrumbs for a more crunchy flavor.

You can use the remaining pickle juice as the vinegar in a brine for chicken wings or fried chicken. If you like to make your own Bloody Mary's or Salad Dressings, you can use in for those recipes as well. For a Greek yogurt spiced up dip, a flavorful coleslaw or seasoned deviled eggs, add a spoonful of pickle juice to the recipe.

Ranch Cucumber Chips

Ingredients:
- 2-3 cucumbers
- 1 Tbsp buttermilk powder
- 1 tsp dried parsley
- 1 tsp dried chives
- 1/2 tsp garlic powder
- 1/2 tsp onion powder
- 1/4 tsp dried dill
- 1 tsp salt
- 1/2 tsp pepper

Directions:
1. Slice the cucumbers into thin and uniform slices.
2. Toss the cucumber slices in 1-2 Tbsp of oil OR vinegar until they are all coated.
3. Place the slices on your dehydrator trays- close but not touching.
4. Mix together all the spices to create your ranch seasoning.
5. Sprinkle spice mixture over all of the cucumbers.
6. Place all 5 racks into the Mojave Air Fryer Dehydrator and set it at 135°F for about 4-6 hours or until completely dry and crisp.
7. Store the cucumber chips in an air tight container so that they retain their crispness. Enjoy!

Air Fryer Zucchini Chips

Servings: 4
Cooking Time: 12 Minutes

Ingredients:
- 1 medium zucchini cut into ½" coins
- 1 beaten egg
- cooking spray
- crumb coating
- ⅔ cup Panko bread crumbs
- ⅔ cup seasoned bread crumbs
- 2 tablespoons Parmesan cheese grated
- 1 teaspoon Italian seasoning

Directions:

1. Preheat air fryer to 375°F.
2. Mix coating ingredients in a bowl.
3. Toss zucchini with egg. Dip zucchini into the coating mixture gently pressing to adhere.
4. Lightly spray zucchini with cooking spray.
5. Place in a single layer in the air fryer basket and cook 6 minutes. Turn zucchini over and air fry 6-8 minutes more or until crisp and zucchini is tender.

NOTES

For batches, undercook zucchini by 2 minutes. Once all batches are cooked, place them all in the air fryer together for 3 minutes to heat through.

Reheat in the air fryer at 375°F for 3-5 minutes or until heated through.

BREAKFAST & BRUNCH RECIPES

The Ultimate Cheese Toastie

Servings: 2
Cooking Time: 6 Minutes

Ingredients:
- 3 Slices sourdough
- 2 Tbsp butter, softened
- 1 Tbsp Dijon mustard
- 6 - 8 slices cheese (mixture of sharp cheddar & mozzarella)
- 2 medium gherkins, sliced
- ½ Red onion, thinly sliced
- 1 Tomato, sliced
- 3 slices of ham or shaved beef

Directions:
1. Thinly spread one side of each bread with butter. To assemble the toastie, place one slice of bread, butter side down and spread half the mustard. Add half the cheese, gherkins, onion, tomato slices and ham. Top with a slice of bread and repeat the sandwich filling finishing off with a slice of bread. Set your air fryer on air fry at 180℃ for 5 minutes.
2. Voila, a delicious cheese toastie by you for you!

Cheesy Breakfast Egg Rolls

Servings: 12
Cooking Time: 10 Minutes

Ingredients:
- 1/2 pound bulk pork sausage
- 1/2 cup shredded sharp cheddar cheese
- 1/2 cup shredded Monterey Jack cheese
- 1 tablespoon chopped green onions
- 4 large eggs
- 1 tablespoon 2% milk
- 1/4 teaspoon salt
- 1/8 teaspoon pepper
- 1 tablespoon butter
- 12 egg roll wrappers
- Cooking spray
- Optional: Maple syrup or salsa

Directions:
1. In a small nonstick skillet, cook sausage over medium heat until no longer pink, 4-6 minutes, breaking it into crumbles; drain. Stir in cheeses and green onions; set aside. Wipe skillet clean.
2. In a small bowl, whisk eggs, milk, salt and pepper until blended. In the same skillet, heat butter over medium heat. Pour in egg mixture; cook and stir until eggs are thickened and no liquid egg remains. Stir in sausage mixture.
3. Preheat air fryer to 400°. With 1 corner of an egg roll wrapper facing you, place 1/4 cup filling just below center of wrapper. (Cover remaining wrappers with a damp paper towel until ready to use.) Fold bottom corner over filling; moisten remaining wrapper edges with water. Fold side corners toward center over filling. Roll egg roll up tightly, pressing at tip to seal. Repeat.
4. In batches, arrange egg rolls in a single layer on greased tray in air-fryer basket; spritz with cooking spray. Cook until lightly browned, 3-4 minutes. Turn; spritz with cooking spray. Cook until golden brown and crisp, 3-4 minutes longer. If desired, serve with maple syrup or salsa.

Air Fryer Hard Boiled Eggs

Servings: 6
Cooking Time: 17 Minutes

Ingredients:
- 6 Eggs

Directions:
1. Place cold eggs into the air fryer basket.
2. Air fry the fresh eggs at 270 degrees Fahrenheit for 17 minutes of cook time.
3. Carefully remove the cooked eggs from the basket of the air fryer and place them into a bowl of ice water.

4. Remove the eggs from the ice water bath after 10 minutes.
5. Carefully remove the outer shell of the egg and serve.

NOTES

Placing the eggs into the ice bath helps bring the temperature of the eggs down, stops the eggs from cooking, and gets them closer to room temperature to make peeling the eggs easier.

Store remaining hard-boiled eggs in an airtight container in the refrigerator for up to 7 days.

Air-fryer Bourbon Bacon Cinnamon Rolls

Servings: 8
Cooking Time: 10 Minutes

Ingredients:

- 8 bacon strips
- 3/4 cup bourbon
- 1 tube (12.4 ounces) refrigerated cinnamon rolls with icing
- 1/2 cup chopped pecans
- 2 tablespoons maple syrup
- 1 teaspoon minced fresh gingerroot

Directions:

1. Place bacon in a shallow dish; add bourbon. Seal and refrigerate overnight. Remove bacon and pat dry; discard bourbon.
2. In a large skillet, cook bacon in batches over medium heat until nearly crisp but still pliable. Remove to paper towels to drain. Discard all but 1 teaspoon drippings.
3. Preheat air fryer to 350°. Separate dough into 8 rolls, reserving icing packet. Unroll spiral rolls into long strips; pat dough to form 6x1-in. strips. Place 1 bacon strip on each strip of dough, trimming bacon as needed; reroll, forming a spiral. Pinch ends to seal. Repeat with remaining dough. Place 4 rolls on ungreased tray in air-fryer basket; cook 5 minutes. Turn rolls over and cook until golden brown, about 4 minutes.
4. Meanwhile, combine pecans and maple syrup. In another bowl, stir ginger together with contents of icing packet. In same skillet, heat remaining bacon drippings over medium heat. Add pecan mixture; cook, stirring frequently, until lightly toasted, 2-3 minutes.
5. Drizzle half the icing over warm cinnamon rolls; top with half the pecans. Repeat to make a second batch.

Air Fryer Waffle Egg In A Hole

Servings: 1
Cooking Time: 8 Minutes

Ingredients:

- 1 frozen waffle
- 1 large egg
- salt and pepper to taste
- 2 tablespoons shredded cheese
- maple syrup to taste

Directions:

1. Preheat the air fryer to 350 degrees F (175 degrees C).
2. Cut a hole in the center of the frozen waffle using the rim of a cup or glass (about 2 to 3 inches in diameter). Move waffle to a square of parchment paper, then carefully place the parchment paper into the preheated air fryer, along with the small center waffle.
3. Crack egg directly into the center of waffle hole; season with salt and pepper to taste. Close the lid and cook until the white of the egg has started to set, about 5 to 6 minutes.
4. Remove small center waffle from the air fryer. Sprinkle shredded cheese onto egg waffle, and cook until the cheese is melted and egg white is completely set, about 1 to 2 minutes.
5. Transfer egg waffle onto a plate; drizzle with maple syrup and serve immediately.

Air Fryer Ranch Breadsticks

Servings: 6

Cooking Time: 10 Minutes

Ingredients:
- 1 can Refrigerated Pizza Dough 13.8 ounces
- 2 tablespoons Hidden Valley Ranch Seasoning
- 2 tablespoons sour cream

Directions:
1. To begin, open can of refrigerated dough and roll into a rectangle shape.
2. In a small bowl, combine the seasoning with the sour cream, and stir together to combine them. Spoon the mixture on top of the rectangle, and spread evenly covering the entire surface.
3. Cut the dough into strips of twelve equal-sized pieces, then fold each strip in half, and twist each piece, pinching the ends of each breadstick. As you twist each piece, they will stretch a little. Just keep them from going longer than the size of your basket or tray.
4. Place the breadsticks in air fryer basket, lined with parchment paper, or lightly sprayed with nonstick cooking spray.
5. Air fry at 350 degrees F for 8-10 minutes, until the breadsticks are golden brown.

NOTES

I make these in my Cosori 5.8 quart air fryer. Because not all air fryer are the same, exact cooking time vary, and may need to be adjusted by 2-3 minutes.

I was able to air fry 6 in each batch of breadsticks. Allow room in the basket for them to expand without overlapping or stacking.

For cheesy breadsticks, you can sprinkle ¼ cup parmesan cheese, mozzarella cheese, or cheddar cheese into the sour cream mixture.

Air Fryer Churros

Servings: 8

Cooking Time: 10 Minutes

Ingredients:
- 1 cup water
- 1/3 cup unsalted butter cut into cubes
- 2 Tbsp granulated sugar
- 1/4 tsp salt
- 1 cup all-purpose flour
- 2 large eggs
- 1 tsp vanilla extract
- oil spray
- Cinnamon-sugar coating:
- 1/2 cup granulated sugar
- 3/4 tsp ground cinnamon

Directions:
1. Put a silicone baking mat on a baking sheet and spray with oil spray.
2. In a medium saucepan add water, butter, sugar, and salt. Bring to a boil over medium-high heat.
3. Reduce heat to medium-low and add flour to the saucepan. Stirring constantly with a rubber spatula cook until the dough comes together and is smooth.
4. Remove from heat and transfer the dough to a mixing bowl. Let cool for 4 minutes.
5. Add eggs and vanilla extract to the mixing bowl and mix using an electric hand mixer or stand mixer until dough comes together. The mixture will look like gluey mashed potatoes. Use your hands to press lumps together into a ball and transfer to a large piping bag fitted with a large star-shaped tip.
6. Pipe churros onto the greased baking mat, into 4-inch lengths and cut end with scissors.
7. Refrigerate piped churros on the baking sheet for 1 hour.
8. Carefully transfer churros with a cookie spatula to the Air Fryer basket, leaving about 1/2-inch space between churros. Spray churros with oil spray. Depending on the size of your Air Fryer you have to fry them in batches.

9. Air fry at 375 degrees F for 10-12 minutes until golden brown.
10. In a shallow bowl combine granulated sugar and cinnamon.
11. Immediately transfer baked churros to the bowl with the sugar mixture and toss to coat. Working in batches. Serve warm with Nutella or chocolate dipping sauce.

Air Fryer Boiled Eggs

Ingredients:
- 6 Eggs
- Bowl of cold water
- Ice

Directions:
1. Place the eggs inside the air fryer basket, leaving a few centimetres between them to allow the air to circulate.
2. Select Air Fry and set the temperature to 132C as per the timings below.
3. Medium Eggs:
4. 8 minutes - Gently set white, and fully liquid yolk - The dippy soldiers egg.
5. 9 minutes - Set white, and soft set, jammy yolks - Perfect for salads!
6. 10 minutes - Set white, near completely set yolk - Great for meal prep, salads and egg mayonnaise sandwiches.
7. 11 minutes - Set white, crumbly yolk - Ideal for Devilled eggs.
8. Large Eggs:
9. 8-9 minutes - Gently set white, and fully liquid yolk - The dippy soldiers egg.
10. 10 minutes - Set white, and soft set, jammy yolks - Perfect for salads!
11. 11 minutes - Set white, near completely set yolk - Great for meal prep, salads and egg mayonnaise sandwiches.
12. 12 minutes - Set white, crumbly yolk - Ideal for Devilled eggs.
13. When the cooking program has finished, remove the eggs from the basket with tongs, and plunge into ice water for 2 minutes to stop them cooking.
14. Serve your eggs as desired.
15. Chefs Tip: If you are peeling the eggs I find lightly cracking the shell with the back of a teaspoon before placing the eggs into the ice water bath makes them easier to peel.

Air Fryer Baked Eggs

Servings: 4
Cooking Time: 25 Minutes

Ingredients:
- 2 x 400g cans chopped tomatoes
- 2 tsp Cooks' Ingredients Peppery Pul Biber
- 1 onion, finely chopped
- 2 clove/s garlic, finely chopped
- 1 red pointed pepper, deseeded and sliced into thin rings
- 4 Waitrose British Blacktail Free Range Medium Eggs
- 1/2 x 25g pack flat-leaf parsley, chopped

Directions:
1. Remove the basket of the air fryer and heat to 180°C. Mix together the chopped tomatoes, pul biber, onion, garlic and red pepper then spoon into the main cooking pan of the air fryer. Cook for 20 minutes, then stir.
2. Open the lid of the air fryer and crack 4 eggs on top of the tomato mixture. Season with freshly ground black pepper and cook for a further 3-4 minutes until the eggs are cooked through to your liking. Scatter with the chopped parsley and serve with crusty bread, if liked.

Cook's tip

Customer safety tips
Follow manufacturer's instructions and advice for specific foods
Pre-heat the air fryer to the correct temperature
If cooking different foods together, be aware that they may require different times and temperatures

Spread food evenly – do not overcrowd pan/chamber
Turn food midway through cooking
Check food is piping/steaming hot and cooked all the way through
Aim for golden colouring – do not overcook

Air Fryer Frozen Pizza Rolls

Servings: 3
Cooking Time: 9 Minutes

Ingredients:

- 18 (170 g) Frozen Pizza Rolls
- optional dipping sauce (marinara, cheese sauce, etc.)
- EQUIPMENT
- Air Fryer

Directions:

1. Place the pizza rolls in the air fryer basket and spread out in to a single even layer. Don't overcrowd the basket or else they won't cook evenly. No oil spray is needed.
2. FOR REGULAR SIZED PIZZA ROLLS:
3. Air Fry at 380°F/193°C for 6-10 minutes or until golden and nearly starting to ooze their filling. Shake and flip over about halfway through cooking.
4. FOR MINI SIZED PIZZA ROLLS:
5. Air Fry at 380°F/193°C for 5-8 minutes or until golden and nearly starting to ooze their filling. Shake and flip over about halfway through cooking.
6. Let them rest for a couple minutes to cool off so the filling isn't dangerously hot. Be careful with that first bite! Serve with optional dipping sauce.

NOTES

Air Frying Tips and Notes:
No Oil Necessary. Cook Frozen - Do not thaw first.
Shake or turn if needed. Don't overcrowd the air fryer basket.
Recipe timing is based on a non-preheated air fryer. If cooking in multiple batches of pizza rolls back to back, the following batches may cook a little quicker.

Recipes were tested in 3.7 to 6 qt. air fryers. If using a larger air fryer, the pizza rolls might cook quicker so adjust cooking time.
Remember to set a timer to shake/flip/toss as directed in recipe.

Air Fryer Hash Browns

Servings: 3-4

Ingredients:

- 3 c. peeled and grated potatoes, preferably russet
- 1/4 c. water
- 1 tbsp. vegetable oil
- 3/4 tsp. salt

Directions:

1. In a medium bowl toss together potatoes and water until the potato is fully coated. Cover with plastic wrap and pierce the plastic with a fork a few times.
2. Transfer to the microwave and cook, pausing to toss the mixture every minute, until the potatoes have almost cooked through but still retain bite, and the mixture has grown starchy and slightly sticky, 3 ½ to 4 minutes.
3. Allow potatoes to cool and then toss with oil and salt. Once ready to handle, form the hash browns into 6 rectangular pucks with rounded edges that are about ¼" thick.
4. Preheat air fryer to 400° and cook until the hash browns are golden brown and crispy, 15 to 20 minutes.

Air Fried Pineapple Empanadas

Ingredients:

- 1 can of crushed pineapple (drain, but keep juice)
- 1 can of pineapple tidbits (drain, but keep juice)
- 1/8 tsp of ground nutmeg
- 1/8 tsp ground ginger
- 1 1/4 tsp of ground cinnamon
- 2 tbsp of white sugar
- Pineapple Juice
- 3 tbsp of cornstarch
- 3 cups of flour

- 2 tsp of baking Powder
- 1/2 tsp of salt
- 1/2 cup of shortening
- 3 eggs
- 1/2 cup of milk

Directions:
1. Filling:
2. Drain can of crushed pineapple
3. Transfer drained pineapple to sauce pan
4. Do the same with can of pineapple tidbits
5. Save juice from both cans of pineapple pieces
6. Add 1/4 tsp of cinnamon, 1/8 tsp of nutmeg, 1/8 of ginger, 1/2 cup of sugar, and 3/4 cup of pineapple juice to saucepan with pineapple chunks
7. Let mixture come to a boil, then cover and let simmer for 45 minutes
8. After filling has simmered, drain excess juice into remaining pineapple juice
9. Allow juice to cool, then add 3 tbsp of cornstarch to cooled juice and mix in well
10. Add the mixture of cornstarch and juice to sauce pan
11. Stir and simmer until thickened. Let cool after the desired consistency has been reached
12. Dough:
13. In a bowl, add 3 cups of flour, 2 tsp of baking powder, 1/2 tsp of salt, 2 tbsp of white sugar, and 1 tsp of cinnamon. Mix well
14. In a separate bowl, mix 2 eggs and 1/2 cup of whole milk
15. Add 1/2 cup of shortening to the first bowl, with the dry ingredients. Then add in the mixture of eggs and milk, blend until it is all combined
16. Knead into 2 spheres, wrap in plastic and refrigerate for 20-30 minutes
17. Empanadas:
18. Lightly beat 1 egg to create egg wash
19. On a floured surface, split dough into 12 balls
20. Roll each ball into a small flat circle
21. Add a dollop of filling
22. Wet bottom edge with egg wash
23. Fold towards you and roll edges to seal
24. Coat in egg wash, pierce holes (allows steam to escape) and sprinkle with raw sugar
25. Add parchment paper and place empanadas in air fryer
26. Set at 320F for 13 minutes
27. Enjoy!
28. Don't forget to share

Air Fryer Cinnamon Rolls

Servings: 8
Cooking Time: 7 Minutes

Ingredients:
- 1 can cinnamon rolls
- icing, whipped cream, or ice cream for topping optional

Directions:
1. Preheat air fryer to 350°F on BAKE.
2. Remove cinnamon buns from the package. Place in the air fryer basket.
3. Cook for 7 minutes or until firm when touched.
4. Top with icing if desired.

Notes

Keep leftover air fryer cinnamon rolls in a covered container at room temperature for up to 2 days. Reheat them in the air fryer on high power.

Air Fryer Potato Pancakes

Servings: 4-6
Cooking Time: 9 Minutes

Ingredients:
- 3 cups of shredded hash browns
- 2-3 green onions
- 1 teaspoon of garlic
- 1 teaspoon of paprika
- Salt and pepper to taste
- 1/4 cup of all purpose flour
- 1 egg

Directions:
1. Combine your shredded hash browns, garlic, paprika, salt and pepper, flour, and egg in a large bowl.

2. Chop your green onions, the green part only, and incorporate them into the mixture.
3. Preheat your air fryer to 370 degrees.
4. While it is preheating, make your pancakes. I took a ¼ cup measuring cup and scooped the mixture into it. I then shook it out and it was formed like the measuring cup. I simply pressed down on the mixture to make it into the pancake form. Once your air fryer is ready, generously spray the bottom of your basket. Lay your potato cakes in the basket. Do not overcrowd it because you will need room to flip them halfway through the cooking time.
5. Cook for 4 minutes and then flip. Spray the tops of your potato pancakes and cook for an additional 4-5 minutes.
6. Serve with a dollop of sour cream and additional green onions, if desired.

NOTES
HOW TO REHEAT POTATO PANCAKES:
Place the potato pancakes in your air fryer.
Air fry for 4-5 minutes or until they are crispy and hot. Serve and enjoy!

Air Fryer Garlic Bread

Servings: 4
Cooking Time: 6 Minutes

Ingredients:
- 1/2 loaf French Bread
- 4 tablespoons butter softened
- 2 tablespoons garlic minced, about 3-4 cloves
- 2 teaspoons dried parsley flakes

Directions:
1. Slice half of a loaf of bread lengthwise. Then cut bread into evenly sized slices. If you are going to use the entire loaf, work in batches as they fit in your air fryer basket, or on your air fryer trays.
2. To make the garlic butter, use a small bowl, combine butter, minced garlic, and parsley flakes. Stir together to evenly distribute the ingredients into the butter.
3. Use a bread knife to spread butter mixture on each slice of bread.
4. Place slices of bread in the air fryer basket and air fry at 370 degrees Fahrenheit for 4-6 minutes, until toast is golden and crispy.

NOTES
Cook times may vary based on type of air fryer oven and wattages.
This garlic bread recipe is for using fresh bread, like a French Loaf, Baguette, or Ciabatta Bread. Depending on the type of bread and thickness of garlic bread slices, you may need to adjust cooking time.

Air Fryer Empanadas

Servings: 4
Cooking Time: 8 Minutes

Ingredients:
- 1 refrigerated pie crust dough
- 1/2 pound lean ground beef
- 1/4 cup yellow onion chopped
- 1 cup frozen mixed vegetables like peas, carrots, and corn
- 1 teaspoon Italian Seasoning
- 1/2 teaspoon salt
- 1/4 teaspoon black pepper
- Egg Wash
- 1 large egg whisked
- 1 tablespoon water

Directions:
1. In a medium pan, over medium-high heat, use a wooden spoon to break up and brown the ground beef, then drain the grease through a strainer.
2. Transfer ground beef mixture to a medium bowl, then add in onion, mixed vegetables, and Italian seasoning, salt and black pepper. Stir together to fully combine, then set aside.
3. Roll out empanada dough on a cutting board and cut circles, about 5-6 inches in diameter. Use a cookie cutter, pastry cutter or biscuit cutter if needed to make the dough rounds the same size.

4. Spoon a small amount of the seasoned ground beef mixture onto one side of the circle. Fold dough over the meat filling, sealing in the mixture, then pinch, or use a fork to seal edges.
5. In a small bowl, whisk together the egg and a tablespoon of water. Use a pastry brush and brush the top of each empanada with egg wash.
6. Place them in the air fryer basket, in a single layer on parchment paper liner, or spritzed with olive oil spray. Air fry at 350 degrees F for 8-10 minutes, until the dough is golden brown.

Sausage & Hash Brown Omelette

Servings: 6

Ingredients:
- 5 eggs
- 60ml whole milk
- flaked sea salt, as desired
- fresh cracked black pepper, as desired
- cooking spray
- 170g pre-cooked, smoked sausage, sliced thin
- 115g grated cheddar cheese
- COOKING MODE
- When entering cooking mode - We will enable your screen to stay 'always on' to avoid any unnecessary interruptions whilst you cook!

Directions:
1. Remove crisper plate from pan. Preheat unit by selecting BAKE, set temperature to 200°C and set time to 3 minutes. Select START/STOP to begin.
2. In a bowl, whisk together the eggs, milk, salt and pepper.
3. After unit has preheated, remove pan from unit and with cooking spray. Pour the egg mixture into the pan.
4. Reinsert pan and cook for 5 minutes. After 5 minutes, remove pan and place sliced sausage evenly on top of eggs, then sprinkle cheese on top. Place frozen chopped hash browns in an even layer on top; reinsert pan.
5. Select BAKE, set temperature to 200°C and set time to 20 minutes. Select START/STOP to begin.
6. When cooking is complete, let rest for 2 minutes. Top with spring onions and serve.
7. TIP Substitute any desired cooked sausage in step 3.

Rustic Mediterranean Tomato Dip With Grilled Pita

Servings: 4

Ingredients:
- 4 pitas
- 8 ounces grape tomatoes
- ⅓ cup kalamata olives, pitted and chopped
- 2 tablespoons pine nuts
- 2 tablespoons fresh mint leaves, chopped
- ½ tablespoon fresh dill, chopped
- 1 teaspoon dried oregano
- 1 garlic clove, very finely minced
- 1 tablespoon red wine vinegar
- 2 tablespoons olive oil, divided
- ½ teaspoon freshly ground black pepper
- Kosher salt, to taste
- 16 ounces labneh

Directions:
1. Place the cooking pot into the base of the Indoor Grill, followed by the grill grate.
2. Select the Air Grill function on low heat, adjust time to 5 minutes, press Shake, then press Start/Pause to preheat.
3. Place the pitas onto the preheated grill grate, then close the lid.
4. Flip the pitas over halfway through the cooking time. The Shake Reminder will let you know when.
5. Remove the pitas and set aside.
6. Place the tomatoes onto the grill grate, then close the lid.
7. Select the Air Grill function on medium heat, adjust time to 6 minutes, press the Preheat button to bypass the preheat function, then press Start/Pause to begin cooking.

8. Transfer the grilled tomatoes to a bowl with the olives, pine nuts, chopped herbs, oregano, garlic, vinegar, 1 tablespoon olive oil, and black pepper. Stir together until combined, then season to taste with kosher salt.
9. Scoop the labneh into a serving bowl, top with the tomato mixture, drizzle with the remaining olive oil, and serve with the pita bread for dipping.

Air Fryer Zucchini Corn Fritters

Servings: 4
Cooking Time: 12 Minutes

Ingredients:
- 2 medium zucchini
- 1 cup corn kernels
- 1 medium potato cooked
- 2 tbsp chickpea flour
- 2-3 garlic finely minced
- 1-2 tsp olive oil
- salt and pepper
- For Serving:
- Ketchup or Yogurt tahini sauce

Directions:
1. Grate zucchini using a grater or food processor. In a mixing bowl, mix grated zucchini with a little salt and leave it for 10-15 min. Then squeeze out excess water from the zucchini using clean hands or using a cheesecloth.
2. Also, grate or mash the cooked potato*.
3. Combine zucchini, potato, corn, chickpea flour, garlic, salt, and pepper in a mixing bowl.
4. Roughly take 2 tablespoon batter, give it a shape of a patty and place them on parchment paper**.
5. Lightly brush oil on the surface of each fritter. Preheat Air Fryer to 360F.
6. Place the fritters on the preheated Air Fryer mesh without touching each other. Cook them for 8 min.
7. Then turn the fritters and cook for another 3-4 min or until well done or till you get the desired color.
8. Serve warm with ketchup or yogurt tahini sauce (see notes to prepare)

Notes
*Cooking potato - cook the potato in a microwave oven for 3 min. Then place in cold water for a few minutes. Peel and then grate or mash it.
**Place the prepared patties on the parchment paper before cooking. It will help to brush the oil and then take it out without breaking or sticking to the bottom. (Please do not put the parchment paper inside the Fryer. The parchment paper is simply to keep the raw fritters before loading them into the Air Fryer)
Add more flour to the batter, if necessary.
For the given quantity of ingredients and using my XL size Philips Air Fryer I cook these fritters in two batches. You can prepare a total of 8 medium to large-size or 12-14 small-size fritters.
For two medium-size zucchini, I could squeeze a little more than ½ cup of water. It is necessary to squeeze out the water as much as possible, to avoid getting mushy or soggy fritters. Also, pat dry, thawed corn kernels if you plan on using frozen ones.
Yogurt tahini sauce - mix ½ cup yogurt with 1 tablespoon tahini and season with salt according to taste.

Air Fryer French Toast

Servings: 4
Cooking Time: 10 Minutes

Ingredients:
- 8 slices brioche bread or other dense bread, thickly sliced
- 4 eggs
- 1 cup milk
- 1 tablespoon sugar
- 1 teaspoon vanilla
- ½ teaspoon cinnamon

Directions:
1. Preheat air fryer to 370°F
2. Whisk eggs, milk, sugar, vanilla, and cinnamon in a shallow bowl or dish.

3. Dip both sides of the bread into the egg mixture allowing a few seconds for the egg to soak into the bread.
4. Place four slices of bread in the air fryer basket and cook for 4 minutes.
5. After four minutes flip the bread and cook for an additional 4-6 minutes or until the bread is golden in color.
6. Repeat with other slices of bread.

Notes

Air Fryers can vary. This recipe was tested in a 5.8QT Cosori. Be sure to check your french toast early so it doesn't overcook and dry out.

Bread Thickness Thicker bread may need a minute extra, thinner bread may need a little bit less time.

Feeding a Crowd? Do not overcrowd the air fryer. If serving a crowd, cook all of the french toast in batches. Once it's all cooked, place it all back into the air fryer and heat for 2 minutes.

Air Fryer Soft Pretzels

Servings: 8
Cooking Time: 14 Minutes

Ingredients:

- 2 1/4 cups all purpose flour
- 1 tsp sugar
- 2 tsps salt
- 1 tbsp dry yeast
- 1 cup warm water
- 2 tbsp unsalted butter melted
- Egg Wash
- 1 large egg
- 1 tsp water

Directions:

1. To prepare your air fryer basket, lightly coat the basket with olive oil, or use air fryer parchment paper liner, set basket aside.
2. In a large bowl, combine the flour, sugar, salt, and yeast.
3. Pour in the warm water and the melted butter, and stir together with a fork until the dough begins to thicken and looks flaky.
4. Remove the dough from the bowl, and on a lightly floured surface, knead the dough until it becomes smooth. Form the dough into a ball shape.
5. Cut the ball of dough into 8 pieces and then roll into ropes.
6. Twist each rope into a pretzel shape and place into the air fryer basket.
7. In a small bowl, whisk the egg with a spoonful of water, brush the top of each pretzel with the egg wash.
8. Air fry at 320 degrees F for 12-14 minutes, until the dough is cooked and the tops are golden brown.

NOTES

Optional Toppings or Dipping Sauces: Melted cheddar cheese, pizza sauce, pepperonis, mozzarella cheese, course salt.

Air Fryer Pretzel Crescent Rolls

Servings: 8

Ingredients:

- 1 quart water
- ¼ cup baking soda
- 1 (8 ounce) package refrigerated crescent roll dough
- pretzel salt
- cooking spray

Directions:

1. Place a large stock pot over high heat. Add water and bring to a boil over high heat.
2. Meanwhile shape crescents into desired shape and preheat air fryer to 350°
3. Preheat an air fryer to 350 degrees F (175 degrees C). Line the air fryer basket with a fitted piece of parchment. Generously spray with cooking spray.
4. Once water is boiling, carefully add baking soda (it WILL bubble up!). Lower crescent rolls into the brine with a spider strainer; boil for 5 seconds.

Transfer onto the parchment paper in the air fryer basket. Sprinkle with salt.

5. Air fry until crescent rolls are cooked through and golden, about 12 minutes. Serve immediately.

Cook's Note:

Not all air fryers operate alike. If you're concerned with the pretzels burning, you CAN follow the same steps and oven bake for 18 to 20 minutes at 350 degrees C (175 degrees C) but it won't have the crispy texture that comes from the air fryer,

Air Fryer Texas Toast

Servings: 8
Cooking Time: 3 Minutes

Ingredients:
- 1 stick salted butter softened ½ cup
- 1 tablespoon olive oil
- 2 cloves garlic minced
- ½ teaspoon dry parsley leaves
- ¼ teaspoon salt
- 8 thick slices of bread 1-inch thick

Directions:
1. Preheat the air fryer to 380°F.
2. In a small bowl mix all ingredients except the bread until smooth.
3. Take each slice of bread and spread the butter mixture on both sides.
4. Place as many slices as will comfortably fit in a single layer into the air fryer basket. Don't overlap.
5. Bake in the air fryer for 2 minutes and then flip. Bake for another minute or until browned.

DESSERTS RECIPES

Hot Cocoa Cookies

Ingredients:
- For the cookies-
- 1/2 cup (1 stick) unsalted butter
- 12 oz. semi-sweet chocolate
- 1 1/2 cups flour
- 1/4 cup unsweetened cocoa powder
- 1 1/2 teaspoons baking powder
- 1/4 teaspoon salt
- 1 1/4 cups brown sugar
- 3 eggs
- 1 1/2 teaspoons vanilla extract
- 15 large marshmallows
- For the icing -
- 2 cups powdered sugar
- 4 tablespoons (1/2 stick) unsalted butter, melted
- 1/4 cup unsweetened cocoa powder
- 1/4 cup hot water
- 1/2 teaspoon vanilla extract
- Assorted sprinkles

Directions:
1. In a medium saucepan (or in a microwave safe bowl, using 50% power), melt the butter and chocolate, stirring frequently. Once melted, set aside to cool slightly.
2. In a medium bowl, whisk together the flour, cocoa powder, baking powder and salt.
3. In the bowl of an electric mixer, beat the sugar, eggs and vanilla on low speed until well combined.
4. Add the cooled chocolate mixture and blend until just combined.
5. While mixing, add the flour mixture slowly and blend until just combined.
6. Scrape down the sides of the bowl, then cover the dough and refrigerate about 1 hour. If making the dough a day ahead, let sit at room temperature for 30 minutes before shaping.
7. Use a tablespoon (or a tablespoon sized cookie scoop) to scoop the dough, then roll the dough in your hands to create balls. Arrange the balls about 2 inches apart on your baking pan, then flatten slightly. Bake cookies in your Air Fryer Oven for about 10 minutes at 320*F.
8. While the cookies bake, cut the large marshmallows in half (crosswise). When the cookies have baked, remove from oven and press one marshmallow half (cut side down) into the center of each cookie. Return the cookies to the oven and bake another 2-3 minutes. Allow the pan of cookies to cool a few minutes, then transfer cookies to cooling rack.
9. Prepare cookie icing by combining all ingredients in a medium bowl and mixing together with a whisk. Place wire cooling rack (with cookies on it) over a baking sheet (to catch any excess icing). Spoon a small amount of icing onto the top of each marshmallow, and use the back of the spoon to spread it a bit. After icing just a couple cookies, top with sprinkles before the icing dries.
10. Allow icing to set up about 30 minutes before serving.

Air Fryer Crab Cakes

Servings: 4
Cooking Time: 10 Minutes

Ingredients:
- 1 large egg whisked
- 1 1/2 tablespoons mayonnaise
- 1/2 teaspoon Dijon mustard
- 1 teaspoon Worcestershire sauce
- 1 teaspoon Old bay seasoning
- 1/4 teaspoon salt
- 1/4 teaspoon pepper
- 1/4 stalk celery finely chopped
- 2 tablespoons parsley finely chopped
- 1/4 small bell pepper finely chopped

- 1/2 lb crab meat canned or fresh
- 1/3 cup panko bread crumbs

Directions:
1. Add all the ingredients, except for the bread crumbs, until combined. Fold through the bread crumbs at the end.
2. Form the mixture into eight crab cakes and place them on a plate lined with parchment paper. Freeze the plate for 5 minutes.
3. Preheat the air fryer to 200C/400F.
4. Grease the air fryer basket and place four crab cakes in it. Air fry for 7-8 minutes, flipping halfway through.
5. Repeat the process until all the crab cakes are cooked.

Notes

TO STORE: In airtight food containers, you can refrigerate leftover crab cakes for up to 5 days.
TO FREEZE: Using freezer-safe bags/ containers and parchment paper, you can freeze them for up to 1 month.
TO REHEAT: Preheat the air fryer to 400°F before putting in the crab cakes. 2 to 3 minutes is enough to reheat them thoroughly.

Air Fryer Apple Fritters

Servings: 4
Cooking Time: 10 Minutes

Ingredients:
- Apple Fritter Recipe
- 2 Granny Smith Apples
- 2 cups All Purpose Flour
- 1/2 cup Granulated White Sugar
- 1 teaspoon Baking Powder
- 1 teaspoon Baking Soda
- 1 teaspoon Cinnamon
- 1 teaspoon Allspice
- 3/4 cup Apple Cider Vinegar
- 2 large Eggs
- 3 Tablespoons Butter
- 1 teaspoon Vanilla Extract
- Sweet Glaze Sauce
- 2 cups Powdered Sugar
- 1/2 teaspoon Cinnamon
- 1/4 cup Milk

Directions:
1. Peel apples and then shred the apples. Spread them over a paper towel or cheesecloth, squeeze out the excess liquid and then pat to absorb moisture.
2. Combine the dry ingredients into a medium bowl and mix in the apples. Mix well.
3. Mix eggs, apple cider, butter, and vanilla in a separate bowl.
4. Fold the flour mixture into the wet ingredients until well combined.
5. Preheat the Air Fryer to 390 degrees Fahrenheit (198 degrees Celsius). Once preheated, place a piece of parchment paper down inside the Air Fryer basket.
6. Use a tablespoon and add dollops of 2 TBSP-sized mixtures to the parchment paper.
7. Spray the with olive oil cooking spray and cook for 6 minutes. Flip the fritters and cook for an additional 4 minutes until golden brown.
8. Whisk the glaze ingredients together and then drizzle over top of the fritters.
9. Serve immediately.

NOTES

Granny Smith Apples: It's tempting to use sweeter apples, but Granny Smith apples are the best apples for this recipe because they're not as juicy and won't make the Air Fryer fritters soggy.
Alternative Flour: You can use almond flour or coconut flour to make an even healthier version of this recipe.
Alternative Sugar: You can substitute maple syrup or brown sugar for the granulated sugar to add a deeper flavor to the fritters.
Cooking spray: You can use olive oil, canola oil, or avocado oil nonstick spray to coat the Air Fryer basket.
Butter: You can use melted butter or softened butter for this recipe. You can also substitute margarine for butter if you like.

Spices: You can add more spices to this classic apple dessert if you want a spicier flavor. For example, you can add nutmeg or cloves, which gives the fritters a more autumnal flavor.

Glaze: If you put too much milk in your glaze, add more powdered sugar. On the other hand, you can add more milk to loosen up the glaze if you put too much powdered sugar. If you prefer a thicker glaze, don't use as much milk. You can also use a splash of half-n-half instead of milk.

This recipe was made with a basket-style 5.8 qt Corsori Air Fryer. If you're using a different brand, you may have to adjust your cooking time accordingly.

Air Fryer Fried Apple Pies

Servings: 8
Cooking Time: 40 Minutes

Ingredients:

- 2 tablespoons butter
- 4 McIntosh apples, peeled, cored, and sliced
- 1/2 cup granulated sugar
- 1/2 teaspoon ground cinnamon
- 1 teaspoon lemon juice
- flour, for dusting
- 1 (8-biscuit) package refrigerated jumbo flaky biscuits
- oil, for spraying
- powdered sugar, for dusting

Directions:

1. To make filling, in a large sauté pan, melt butter. Add apples, granulated sugar, cinnamon, and lemon juice. Sauté over medium heat until apples are soft, about 15 minutes. Remove from heat and cool.
2. On a lightly floured surface, roll out biscuits into 7- to 8-inch-diameter circles. Place 2 or 3 tablespoons of the apple filling on each circle and brush edges with water. Fold half of each circle over filling to make a half-moon shape. Seal by pressing edges with tines of a fork.
3. Working in batches of 2, spray pies on both sides with oil and place in air fryer basket lined with parchment paper. Set air fryer temperature to 350 degrees, and air fry for 5 minutes. Flip pies, spray with oil, and air fry for 5 minutes more. Repeat with remaining pies. Dust pies with powdered sugar.

NOTES

For quick and easy pies, use one 21-ounce can apple pie filling instead of making your own.

Homemade Bagels

Servings: 4-6
Cooking Time: 20 Minutes

Ingredients:

- 1 1/2 cups Warm Water
- 2 1/2 tsp Instant Yeast
- 4 1/4 cups Flour (Bread or Self Raising)
- 1 Tbsp sugar
- 2 tsp salt
- 1/4 cup milk
- Seeds e.g sesame – optional
- Toppings:
- Smoked salmon, cream cheese, or for breakfast For breakfast bagels I love serving it with avocado, poached eggs, ham & hollandaise sauce.

Directions:

1. Add the yeast to the warm water and let it stand for 5 minutes to activate.
2. Slowly mix in the flour, sugar and salt and massage together until a dough forms. You can use a stand mixer or just mix with a wooden spoon. Once a dough forms, use your hands to knead the dough until pliable.
3. Once kneaded, insert the inner pot, place the dough inside and switch on to Keep Warm mode or Yogurt mode and set time for 60 min. Cover with the lid or a cloth. Once the Instant Pot beeps, remove lid and dough which will have risen. Remove the dough and cut into equal size pieces. Then roll into small fist size balls. Push your finger

into the centre of each ball to make the hole and form the bagels.
4. Wipe down the inner pot and then add 4 cups of water, set to Sauté mode and bring to a boil. Once the water is boiling, keep it at a rolling boil and add the bagels to boil for 1 minute. Then gently remove and set aside to dry. Brush with milk and add your seeds of choice.
5. If using a Duo Crisp, swop the lids to Air Fry lid and insert the air fry basket. Set to Bake at 200c for 10 mins turning half way. For the Vortex insert into the inner basket and use the same temperature and time settings.
6. The bagels will be a beautiful golden colour when done! Serve with fillings of your choice. For breakfast bagels I love serving it with avocado, poached eggs, ham & hollandaise sauce.
7. Enjoy!

Air Fryer Basic Vanilla Butter Cookies

Servings: 15
Cooking Time: 40 Minutes

Ingredients:
- 125 grams butter, softened
- ½ cup (110g) caster sugar
- 1 teaspoon vanilla extract
- 1 egg yolk
- 1¼ cups (185g) plain flour
- 2 tablespoon caster sugar, extra
- to serve: icing sugar

Directions:
1. Beat butter, sugar and vanilla in a small bowl with an electric mixer until light and fluffy. Beat in egg yolk until combined. Sift flour, in two batches, into butter mixture; mix well.
2. Knead dough on a lightly floured surface until smooth. Using your hands, shape dough into a 25cm long log. Place extra caster sugar on a plate; roll log in the sugar. Wrap log in baking paper. Freeze for 1 hour or until firm.
3. Remove log from the freezer. Stand for 10 minutes. Slice into 15 x 1.5cm thick rounds.
4. Preheat a 7-litre air fryer to 160°C/325°F for 5 minutes.
5. Taking care, line the air fryer basket with baking paper. Place half the cookies, 2cm apart, in the basket (place remaining cookies in the fridge until needed); at 160°C/350°F, cook for 12 minutes until golden. Remove the basket from the pan. Cool cookies in the basket for 10 minutes before transferring to a wire rack to cool completely. Repeat cooking with remaining cookies.
6. Dust cookies with icing sugar.

Notes
Cookies will keep in an airtight container for up to 2 weeks.

Air Fryer Blueberry Cheesecake Wontons

Servings: 4
Cooking Time: 6 Minutes

Ingredients:
- 4 ounces cream cheese softened
- 1 tbsp granulated sugar
- ½ tsp vanilla
- 1 tbsp sour cream
- ¼ cup blueberries fresh or frozen, cut into half if larger in size
- 8-12 wonton wrappers 3x3 inches
- ¼ cup powdered sugar

Directions:
1. In a medium bowl, combine cream cheese, sugar, sour cream and vanilla. Stir together until well blended and smooth. Add blueberries and gently fold into the cream cheese mixture.
2. Lay wonton wrappers flat, and spoon a small amount of the mixture into the center of the wonton. Brush the edges of the wonton wrapper with water and then bring sides together to make a small pillow shape square.

3. Place filled wontons in a lightly sprayed air fryer basket, without stacking or overlapping. Lightly spray the wontons with olive oil spray to help with crispness and color.
4. Air fry at 350 degrees F for 6-8 minutes until wontons are golden and crispy.
5. Remove from the air fryer basket and sprinkle with a light dusting of powdered sugar.

Air Fryer Cranberry Brie Bites

Servings: 7
Cooking Time: 3 Minutes

Ingredients:
- 1 package baked phyllo cups
- 1 can cranberry sauce (you will only use about half)
- 1/2 wheel brie cheese 4 ounces

Directions:
1. Cube the cheese into pieces. Gently press a brie piece into the cup with a spoon or using your fingers. Cut a bite size piece for each cup, which is about 1-inch cubes.
2. Once the cups have been lined with cheese, top the brie with cranberry sauce. I used about a teaspoon of cranberry sauce on each piece.
3. Place the cups in the air fryer basket or on a small baking sheet. Air Fry at 300 degrees Fahrenheit for 3-5 minutes, until golden brown. If they aren't warm, add an additional 1-2 minutes.

NOTES
Baked brie tastes best if served warm.
You can sprinkle brown sugar on top before cooking, or add a teaspoon of brown sugar to the cranberry sauce before baking.
For an extra splash of seasonal colors for a festive appetizer, garnish with a sprig of fresh rosemary.

Soufflé Pancakes With Berries & Cream

Servings: 6

Ingredients:
- 1½ cups all-purpose flour
- 4 tablespoons powdered sugar, divided, plus more for dusting
- 2 teaspoons baking powder
- ½ teaspoon kosher salt
- 1¼ cups whole milk
- 4 tablespoons unsalted butter, melted
- 1 large egg yolk
- ½ teaspoon vanilla extract
- 4 large egg whites
- ¾ teaspoon cream of tartar
- 1 cup heavy whipping cream
- 1 teaspoon vanilla extract
- Oil spray
- Fresh berries, for serving
- Items Needed:
- Stand mixer fitted with whisk attachment
- Silicone or rubber spatula
- 2 ring molds (3–4 inch diameter)

Directions:
1. Whisk the flour, 2 tablespoons of powdered sugar, baking powder, and salt together in a large bowl. Set aside.
2. Whisk the milk, melted butter, egg yolk, and vanilla extract together in a medium bowl, then stir into the dry ingredients until just combined.
3. Place the egg whites and cream of tartar in the bowl of a stand mixer fitted with the whisk attachment. Whisk on high speed until stiff peaks form, about 4 minutes.
4. Fold the egg white mixture into the batter in two additions using a silicone or rubber spatula until just combined, being careful not to pop the air bubbles. Set aside.
5. Place the heavy cream, remaining powdered sugar, and vanilla extract in the bowl of the stand mixer

and beat until stiff peaks form to make the whipped cream. Refrigerate until ready to use.

6. Remove the crisper plate from the Smart Air Fryer.
7. Set temperature to 330°F and time to 3 minutes, then press Start/Pause to preheat the air fryer.
8. Spray the inside of the ring molds with oil spray.
9. Spray the air fryer basket with oil spray, then place the ring molds directly into the basket without the crisper plate and fill them to the top with pancake batter.
10. Set temperature to 330°F and time to 3 minutes, then press Start/Pause.
11. Flip the pancakes over while still in the ring molds when the timer goes off.
12. Set temperature to 330°F and time to 2 minutes, then press Start/Pause.
13. Remove the pancakes when done, and repeat the cooking process with the remaining batter.
14. Serve with a dollop of whipped cream, a dusting of powdered sugar, and fresh berries.

Apple Cider Donuts

Servings: 18
Cooking Time: 45 Minutes

Ingredients:
- FOR THE DONUTS:
- 2 cups apple cider
- 3 cups all-purpose flour
- 1/2 cup packed light brown sugar
- 2 teaspoons baking powder
- 1 teaspoon ground cinnamon
- 1 teaspoon ground ginger
- 1/2 teaspoon baking soda
- 1/2 teaspoon kosher salt
- 8 tablespoons (1 stick) cold unsalted butter
- 1/2 cup cold milk
- FOR SHAPING AND FINISHING:
- 1/4 cup all-purpose flour
- 8 tablespoons unsalted butter
- 1 cup granulated sugar
- 1 teaspoon ground cinnamon

Directions:
1. Make the dough: Pour 2 cups apple cider into a small saucepan and bring to a boil over medium-high heat. Boil until reduced by half (to 1 cup), 10 to 12 minutes. Err on the side of over-reducing (you can always add a little bit extra apple cider to the reduced amount). Transfer the cider reduction to a heatproof measuring cup and cool completely, about 30 minutes.
2. Place 3 cups all-purpose flour, 1/2 cup packed light brown sugar, 2 teaspoons baking powder, 1 teaspoon ground cinnamon, 1 teaspoon ground ginger, 1/2 teaspoon baking soda, and 1/2 teaspoon kosher salt in a large bowl and whisk to combine.
3. Grate 8 tablespoons cold unsalted butter on the large holes of a box grater. Add the grated butter to the flour mixture and use your fingers to incorporate the butter until it is about the texture of small pebbles. Make a well in the center of mixture. Add the 1 cup reduced cider and 1/2 cup cold milk to the well and use a wide spatula to mix the dough together.
4. Shape the dough: Sprinkle a work surface with a few tablespoons of flour. Place the dough on the flour. Pat the dough into an even layer about 1-inch thick, and sprinkle with more flour. Fold the dough onto itself and pat it down until 1-inch thick. Fold and pat again, repeating about 6 times, until the dough is slightly springy. Pat the dough into a rough 9x13-inch rectangle about 1/2-inch thick.
5. Cut donuts out of the dough with a floured donut cutter (or a 3-inch and 1-inch round cutter). You should get about 8 donuts out of the first round of cutting. Transfer the donuts to a baking sheet. Gather the scraps, pat the dough down again, and repeat cutting until you have about 18 donuts. Refrigerate the donuts while you preheat the air fryer to 375°F for about 10 minutes. Meanwhile, prepare the coating.
6. Melt the remaining 8 tablespoons of butter and place in a medium bowl. Place 1 cup granulated

sugar and 1 teaspoon ground cinnamon in a small bowl and whisk together with a fork.

7. Depending on the size of your air fryer, air fry in batches of 3 to 4 at a time, flipping them halfway through, 12 minutes per batch. Transfer the donuts to a wire rack and load the air fryer with the next batch. Meanwhile, dip the fried donuts first in the butter, and then the cinnamon sugar. Place back on the wire rack. Serve the donuts warm or at room temperature with warm cider for dipping.

NOTES

Make ahead: The dough can be mixed and folded the night before. Store tightly wrapped in the fridge and bring to room temperature for 30 minutes before punching out the donut shape and air frying.

Storage: These donuts are best made the day they are made, but leftovers keep well for up to 2 days in a tightly sealed container at room temperature.

How To Toast A Bagel In An Air Fryer

Servings: 2
Cooking Time: 3 Minutes

Ingredients:
- 2 bagels

Directions:
1. To make the perfect air fryer toasted bagel, being by slicing 2 standard-sized sliced bagels in half and place into the air fryer basket, in a single layer, cut side up.
2. Air fry at 380 degrees for 3-4 minutes, until golden brown and crispy. Depending on the crispness you prefer, use 2-3 minutes for lightly crispy, and 3-4 minutes for darker crisp.
3. Top with your favorite toppings such as cream cheese or a bit of butter.

Air Fryer Oven Slime-filled Cookies

Ingredients:
- 1 1/2 cups salted butter, room temperature
- 1 cup brown sugar
- 1 cup white sugar
- 2 eggs
- 2 tsp vanilla extract
- 2 1/2 cups all-purpose flour
- 1 cup cocoa powder
- 1/4 cup baking powder
- Black food coloring
- 32 green gummy candies
- Edible eye candies OR white icing and black sprinkles

Directions:
1. In a large mixing bowl, cream together room temperature butter and sugar until well combined and slightly fluffy. Mix in eggs and vanilla.
2. Add flour, cocoa, and baking powder gradually, continuing to mix until well incorporated.
3. Make balls of dough about 2 Tbsp. in size. Break in half and add gummy candy. Seal edges back together,
4. Cover wire racks with tinfoil. Perforate to allow air flow. Place dough balls about 2-inches apart. If using, add candy eyes to the top of each.
5. Bake for 5 minutes at 350. Allow to cool slightly Decorate with icing and sprinkles, if needed. Enjoy!

Crispy Air Fryer Apple Fritters

Servings: 10
Cooking Time: 6 Minutes

Ingredients:
- 225g self-raising flour
- 80 g castor sugar
- Pinch of salt
- Pinch of cinnamon
- ½ cup apple juice
- 30 g melted butter
- 2 eggs

- 1 tsp vanilla essence
- 2 apples grated

Directions:
1. Sift the flour into a bowl add the sugar, cinnamon & salt.
2. Add the apple juice, vanilla essence, butter & lightly whisked eggs.
3. Add the grated apple.
4. Mix until the ingredients come together.
5. Place baking paper on the vortex baking tray make sure to leave 1 cm space between the edge of the tray to allow air flow.
6. Spray the paper with cooking spray.
7. Spoon the mixture onto the baking sheets.
8. Set the Vortex Oven (can also use Vortex, Vortex Plus and Duo Crisp) to Bake at 200°c for 6 mins. turn halfway through the cooking process.
9. When you remove them from the oven toss in cinnamon and sugar.
10. Serve with custard or vanilla ice cream.

Best-ever S'mores

Servings: 4

Ingredients:
- FOR CAMPFIRE
- 4 whole graham crackers
- 4 marshmallows
- 4 pieces chocolate (such as Hershey's)
- FOR AIR FRYER
- 4 whole graham crackers
- 2 marshmallows
- 4 pieces chocolate (such as Hershey's)

Directions:
1. FOR CAMPFIRE:
2. Break all graham crackers in half to create 8 squares. Place one square of chocolate on 4 graham squares.
3. Place marshmallows on skewer or marshmallow roasting stick. Roast over open flame or grill until toasted to your preference.
4. Transfer marshmallow onto graham cracker with chocolate, then top with second graham cracker square.
5. FOR AIR FRYER:
6. Break all graham crackers in half to create 8 squares. Cut marshmallows in half crosswise with a pair of scissors.
7. Place marshmallows cut side down on 4 graham squares. Place marshmallow side up in basket of air fryer and cook on 390° for 4 to 5 minutes, or until golden.
8. Remove from air fryer and place a piece of chocolate and graham square on top of each toasted marshmallow and serve.

Peanut Butter Explosion Cakes

Servings: 4

Ingredients:
- 1/2 c. (1 stick) butter, cut into cubes, plus more for ramekins
- 1 c. chocolate chips
- 1/2 c. powdered sugar, plus more for topping
- 2 large eggs, plus 2 egg yolks
- 1 tsp. pure vanilla extract
- 1/4 c. unsweetened cocoa powder
- 1/4 c. all-purpose flour
- 1/2 tsp. kosher salt
- 4 tbsp. peanut butter
- 1 c. water

Directions:
1. FOR THE INSTANT POT:
2. Grease 4 ramekins with butter. In a medium microwave-safe bowl, combine butter and chocolate chips and melt in 30-second intervals until melted. Add powdered sugar, eggs, egg yolks, and vanilla and whisk until smooth. Add cocoa powder, flour, and salt and whisk until just combined.
3. Pour ramekins only halfway with batter, then top each ramekin with about 1 heaping tablespoon of

peanut butter. Top with remaining batter. Cover ramekins tightly with foil.

4. Place trivet inside Instant Pot and pour in water. Place 3 ramekins on trivet and stack fourth one in center on top. Lock lid and Pressure Cook on High for 20 minutes.
5. Follow manufacturer's instructions for quick release and, using tongs, carefully remove ramekins from Instant Pot. Uncover and run a knife or offset spatula around edges. Invert onto plate, then dust with powdered sugar before serving.
6. FOR THE AIR FRYER:
7. Grease 4 ramekins with butter. In a medium microwave-safe bowl, combine butter and chocolate chips and melt in 30-second intervals until melted. Add powdered sugar, eggs, egg yolks, and vanilla and whisk until smooth. Add cocoa powder, flour, and salt and whisk until just combined.
8. Pour ramekins only halfway with batter, then top each ramekin with about 1 heaping tablespoon of peanut butter. Top with remaining batter. Cover ramekins tightly with foil.
9. Place ramekins in air fryer basket, working in batches if necessary. Cook at 375° for 12 minutes, remove foil, and cook for 6 minutes more.
10. Carefully remove ramekins from air fryer; run a knife or offset spatula around edges. Invert onto plate, then dust with powdered sugar before serving.

Air Fried Cheese Curds

Servings: 4
Cooking Time: 4 Minutes

Ingredients:
- 8 ounces cheese curds
- ⅓ cup flour
- 1 large egg
- 1 cups panko bread crumbs
- 1 teaspoon garlic powder
- ¼ teaspoon smoked paprika

Directions:
1. Preheat air fryer to 400°F.
2. Crack egg into a small bowl. Place bread crumbs and seasonings in another bowl.
3. Place cheese curds in third bowl and toss with flour. Remove from the flour allowing excess to fall off and toss with egg.
4. Dip the cheese curds in the crumb mixture gently pressing to adhere. Repeat with remaining curds and place on a baking sheet.
5. Freeze cheese curds for 30 minutes before cooking, once frozen generously spray curds with cooking spray.
6. Place in a single layer in the preheated basket and cook 3-4 minutes or until crisp and melted.

Notes
Important: Cheese curds must be frozen before cooking or they will not crisp on the outside before melting.

Don't overcook them, they should be just melted and crisp on the outside.

The cheese curds can be prepared and frozen for several months for a quick snack at any time!

Air Fryer Donuts

Servings: 8
Cooking Time: 7 Minutes

Ingredients:
- 1 3/4 cup self rising flour
- 1 cup vanilla yogurt
- For the glaze
- 1 1/2 cups powdered sugar sifted
- 1-2 tablespoons water or milk
- 2 tablespoons rainbow sprinkles optional

Directions:
1. In a large mixing bowl, add your flour and yogurt and mix well, until a thick dough remains. If the dough is too thin, add more flour. If the dough is too thick, add more yogurt.

2. Lightly flour a kitchen surface and transfer the dough onto it. Knead it several times until smooth. Divide the dough into 8 equal portions. Roll out each portion of dough into a long, sausage shape and connect both sides to form a donut.
3. Line an air fryer basket with parchment paper. Place 2-4 donuts on them (depending on how big your air fryer is), ensuring the donuts are at least half an inch apart, to ensure they have room to rise and spread.
4. Air fry the donuts at 200C/400F for 7-8 minutes, or until firm on the outside. Repeat the process until all the donuts are cooked.
5. Let the donuts cool completely. While cooling, prepare the glaze. Sift the powdered sugar into a large bowl. Add 1-2 tablespoons of water (or milk) and mix until a thick and smooth glaze remains.
6. Dip each donut in the glaze and place them on a wire rack. If desired, top with sprinkles.

Notes

TO STORE: Leftover donuts can be stored in the refrigerator, covered, for up to five days.
TO FREEZE: Place the donuts in an airtight container and store them in the freezer for up to six months.

Air Fryer Bagels

Servings: 8
Cooking Time: 10 Minutes

Ingredients:
- 1 3/4 cups self rising flour
- 1 cup Greek yogurt
- 1 tablespoon butter melted
- 1 tablespoon sesame seeds or favorite bagel toppings

Directions:
1. In a large mixing bowl, add the flour and yogurt and mix until combined. If the dough is too thin, add more flour. If the dough is too thick, add more yogurt.
2. Lightly flour a kitchen surface and transfer the dough on top. Knead it several times, then divide it into 8 portions.
3. Roll out each portion of dough into a long, sausage shape and connect them at both sides to form a bagel.
4. Line an air fryer basket with parchment paper. Brush the top of the bagel with the melted butter then sprinkle your favorite bagel toppings.
5. Place 3 or 4 bagels in the air fryer basket and air fry at 180C/350F for 10 minutes, or until golden around the sides.
6. Remove the bagels from the air fryer basket and place the remaining bagels to cook. Repeat the process until all the bagels are air fried.

Notes

TO STORE: Air fried bagels can be stored in the refrigerator, covered, for up to 5 days.
TO FREEZE: Place leftovers in a ziplock bag and store them in the freezer for up to six months.
TO REHEAT: Microwave for 20-30 seconds or reheat in the air fryer for 1-2 minutes.

Frozen Waffles In The Air Fryer

Servings: 2
Cooking Time: 3 Minutes

Ingredients:
- 4 frozen Eggo waffles
- Butter, maple syrup, fresh fruit, or your favorite waffle toppings

Directions:
1. Place frozen waffles in the air fryer basket. They can overlap a little bit!
2. Air fry waffles in the air fryer at 360 degrees F for 3 minutes, flip, then cook for another 1-2 minutes until crispy to your liking. Serve immediately with your favorite toppings.

NOTES

HOW TO REHEAT WAFFLES:
Place waffles in your air fryer.
Heat at 360 degrees until hot & crispy.

Air Fryer Pecan Pie

Servings: 8
Cooking Time: 30 Minutes

Ingredients:

- 1 cup light corn syrup
- 1 cup brown sugar
- 1/3 cup butter melted
- 2 tsp vanilla
- 1/2 tsp salt
- 3 large eggs
- 1 1/2 cups chopped pecans
- 1 pie crust

Directions:

1. Prepare the crust and place into a pie plate that will fit into your basket or rack oven. Air fry the crust at 320 degrees F for 3-4 minutes, then remove until the filling is ready
2. In a medium bowl, pour in the corn syrup, brown sugar, melted butter, vanilla, and salt. Stir all of the ingredients together so the sugar is mixed into the liquids.
3. Whisk or beat the eggs, and add whisked eggs to the bowl. Next, add the pecans and stir into the egg mixture. Once it is well combined, pour into the prepared crust.
4. Place in the air fryer basket, or on the rack, and air fry at 350 degrees F for about 30-35 minutes, until the top of the pie is golden brown and crispy.

NOTES

If the top of the pie begins to darken before cooking time is done, cover with foil.

Chocolate Hot Cross Buns

Servings: 16

Ingredients:

- For the buns:
- 280ml milk
- 70g butter
- 60g sugar
- 10g instant yeast
- 1 large egg
- 5ml vanilla extract
- 450g white bread flour
- 20g cocoa
- 5ml salt
- 5ml cinnamon
- 5ml mixed spice
- 20ml mixed candied citrus peel (4 tsp)
- 50g dark chocolate
- 50g milk chocolate
- 50g white chocolate
- For the glaze:
- 30ml sugar (2 tbsp)
- 30ml boiling water (2 tbsp)
- For the crosses:
- 80g white chocolate

Directions:

1. Heat the milk, butter and sugar together until the butter has melted and the mixture is lukewarm. Sprinkle the yeast on top, mix well and leave to stand for a few minutes. Place the flour, cocoa, salt and spices into the bowl of your stand mixer. Make a well in the centre, then add in the milk and yeast mixture as well as the egg and vanilla extract. Use the dough hook to mix together until a soft dough has formed. Continue mixing for 5 minutes until the dough starts "climbing" the dough hook. Scoop the dough onto a floured surface and kneading by hand for a further 2 minutes. If you don't have a stand mixer, use a wooden spoon to blend the ingredients together and knead the dough for 10 minutes by hand. Place the dough into a lightly oiled bowl and cover with oiled clingfilm. Leave in a warm place for 1 hour, or until the dough has doubled in volume. Punch down the dough, and add the mixed citrus peel and finely chopped dark, milk and white chocolate. Knead the dough well to distribute the chocolate evenly.
2. Divide the dough in half, then cut each half into 8 equal pieces of dough. Roll the pieces of dough into balls. Lightly grease a 19cm round baking tin. Place 1 ball of dough in the middle, and then 7 around it. Repeat with the remaining dough so that you have 2 tins with 8 buns in each. Cover both with lightly oiled clingfilm and leave to rise for a further 30

minutes. Set the Instant Vortex Air Fryer to 165°C and 20 minutes. When the Airfryer has pre-heated, bake the hot cross buns, one tin at a time. Meanwhile make the glaze by mixing the sugar and water together until the sugar is completely dissolved. Brush the buns with the sugar glaze while they are still hot, then leave to cool for 10 minutes in the tin. Place on a cooling rack to cool completely. For the crosses, finely chop the white chocolate, then place in a heatproof bowl and melt in the microwave at 15 second intervals (or over a pan of hot water). Place the melted white chocolate into a piping bag, then pipe a cross onto each bun. These are best enjoyed fresh on the day you make them, but are also delicious when halved and toasted in the Instant Vortex Air Fryer 200°C for 3 minutes (pipe the white chocolate crosses on after toasting!).

Red Velvet Cookies

Servings: 30

Ingredients:

- 2 c. all-purpose flour
- 1/2 c. Dutch process cocoa powder
- 1 tsp. baking soda
- 1 tsp. kosher salt
- 1 c. (2 sticks) unsalted butter, at room temperature
- 3/4 c. packed brown sugar
- 1/2 c. granulated sugar
- 1 large egg
- 1 tsp. red gel paste food coloring
- 2 tsp. pure vanilla extract
- 1 12-oz pkg semisweet chocolate chips

Directions:

1. Heat oven to 350°F. Line baking sheets with parchment paper. In large bowl, whisk together flour, cocoa, baking soda and salt.
2. Using electric mixer on medium speed, beat together butter and sugars until combined. Add egg, food coloring and vanilla and mix until just combined.
3. Reduce mixer speed to low and add flour mixture until just combined. Fold in chocolate chips.
4. Scoop heaping spoonfuls of dough onto prepared sheets, spacing 1½ inches apart.
5. Bake cookies, rotating positions of pans on racks halfway through, until darker around edges, 9 to 12 minutes total.
6. Let cool 5 minutes on pans, then slide parchment (and cookies) onto wire rack and let cool at least 5 minutes more before serving.
7. AIR FRYER:
8. Line air-fryer basket with a piece of parchment paper, leaving enough space along the edges to allow for air circulation. Heat air fryer to 300°F. Scoop 2 tablespoons of dough per cookie. Working in batches if needed, place cookies 2 inches apart on parchment-lined air-fryer basket. Air-fry until cookies are set and tops are slightly cracked, 14 to 15 minutes. Remove cookies from air fryer immediately and let set for 5 minutes, then transfer to wire rack to cool completely.

Carnival Fried Oreos

Ingredients:

- Crescent roll dough
- Oreos
- Powdered sugar, for topping
- Optional: any other sweet dipping sauces

Directions:

1. Pop the crescent sheet roll and spread it on the table. The dough will be perforated already to make 8 crescents. Cut each triangle in half. One pack of dough will be enough for 16 Oreos.
2. Wrap the Oreo cookies. Mold and form the dough to cover the entire cookie.
3. Place your prepared cookies in the air fryer basket lined with perforated parchment paper (optional). Air fry at 360°F for 2 minutes. Flip them over and cook for another 2 minutes.
4. Sprinkle with powdered sugar or pair with your favorite sweet dipping sauce and enjoy!

Printed in Great Britain
by Amazon